AN AUDACIOUS QUEST!

To save the incomparably lovely Princess Alandra—the innocent, the pure, the very embodiment of the magic that will meld the world's contrasting and chaotic forces, the Key to the forces of Good . . . or is she?

THE REDOUBTABLE QUESTERS!

Mullshire's finest Knights—brave, powerful, skilled in all manner of armament, paragons of virtue, each and every one . . . and arrogant, stupid, and never tested in battle.

IAN FARTHING

The Magic Cobbler who fell from the sky . . . companion to knights, he's afraid of the dark, the light, and becoming a hero.

AND THE WRAITH BOARD ITSELF

Home to assorted man and woman-eating trolls, monsters, a Hag, Magicians, an entire bestiary of beasties—and the one being who knows how to use the Key to destroy every level of the Multiverse!

WRAITH BOARD

BOOK TWO

of

THE GAMING MAGI

DAVID BISCHOFF

A SIGNET BOOK

NEW AMERICAN LIBRARY

*This is for my sisters-in-law
Nikki and Terry Bischoff*

NAL BOOKS ARE AVAILABLE AT QUANTITY DISCOUNTS
WHEN USED TO PROMOTE PRODUCTS OR SERVICES.
FOR INFORMATION PLEASE WRITE TO PREMIUM MARKETING DIVISION,
NEW AMERICAN LIBRARY, 1633 BROADWAY,
NEW YORK, NEW YORK 10019.

Copyright © 1985 by David Bischoff

All rights reserved

Cover art by Kenuko Craft

SIGNET TRADEMARK REG. U.S. PAT. OFF. AND FOREIGN COUNTRIES
REGISTERED TRADEMARK—MARCA REGISTRADA
HECHO EN CHICAGO, U.S.A.

SIGNET, SIGNET CLASSIC, MENTOR, PLUME, MERIDIAN AND NAL BOOKS
are published by New American Library,
1633 Broadway, New York, New York 10019

First Printing, July, 1985

1 2 3 4 5 6 7 8 9

PRINTED IN THE UNITED STATES OF AMERICA

. . . and as to the place called the Dark Circle by some, the Magic Hole by others, and Hell by the less imaginative, the given reason, my dear Wordworm, for that Maelstrom of Magicality, that Cyclone of Uncertainty, was of course for its "pressure-valve" properties. In case your vaunted whimsical memory serves you in its usual fashion, I shall reiterate the situation as outlined by me before the Council:

The sudden boom of creation initiated by the various Games had set into motion an alarming number of intersecting universes, separated only by the flimsiest of membranes. Had these universes been of a homogeneous nature—i.e., equipped with the same laws physical, magical and spiritual—there would have been no problem. However, because of the ephemeral and—let's face it—lamebrain nature of most of them and the strain between them, to say nothing of the vacuum created when one simply popped away into the nothingness, border lines occasionally dissolved, placing sea monsters in Scottish lochs or Cossacks in Fairyland and causing no end of headache for the Overseers who maintained the Equilibrium. My notion of a Netherland as a locus for all borders, a place where everything and anything was allowable, to serve as a kind of magnet for improbabilities that might otherwise be hurled from their home universe into alien and unwelcoming territory, was the perfect solution.

5

And why? Perhaps mainly because much of the excess energy generated by the friction between universes was thus safely dissipated and the "integrity" (read "status quo") could be maintained.

But of course I had other reasons. I had long grown bored with playing the Games in the separate universes—the imaginations of most of the players were so frightfully boring, and their escapades so dull—and I longed for a wilder, more exciting board for my capers and famed escapades. Of course, by now the cretins have infiltrated the territory of my devising with their plodding methodologies, strategies, and mathematical tables, taking all the fun out once more, and I dream of a different board, a restructuring to allow for the improvisations of delight and innovation to once more direct the paths of Gaming.

Something I call the Wraith Board. I trust you will find my suggestions to your liking, since I do need your support in this matter.

Yes, and other reasons for the initial suggestion, my dear dear Wordworm . . .

Have I ever mentioned to you where that dissipated energy goes?

—Excerpt from letter
by Lord Colin
Rawlings to Lord
Scriptus Wordworm

chapter one

Ian Farthing stumped back toward the campsite, bearing a load of the driest firewood he could find. Dusk was just seeping toward full night, and the swaths of shadow had all filled into a terrible darkness. A wind rattled tree branches, swept dead leaves up into the lad's face, drove snatches of cemetery smell at him in clumps of cold and damp.

Damn, thought Ian. Where were they? Had he ranged too far away from the others and gotten himself jolly well lost?

Wind through moonlit bushes whispered: "Yessss . . . yesss . . . you stupid . . . idiot."

Or seemed to, anyway. Ian shivered, and his teeth rattled involuntarily. He dropped a dead branch, thought about it a moment, and then decided to just let it lie. What good would firewood do for Hillary and the questing knights if he couldn't find them? And what good would a twisted cobbler's son do in the rescue of Princess Alandra if he got lost in the woods of the Dark Circle and got himself eaten by a fangamorph, or dragged to hell by a grue, or otherwise unpleasantly rearranged by one of the death-minded denizens?

No, a lost faggot was small sacrifice. A little chill could be borne this night by his living body—death was far colder.

He stopped for a moment and strained his ears for some sign of his fellows. Were those voices he heard?

No, just more wind sounds. But he was going in the right direction, dammit, he was sure of it! He'd just wandered farther afield than he'd thought.

One of the moons broke through a batch of cloud, brightening matters a bit. Ian looked around to get his bearings and paused a moment to ponder that moon.

This moon, like its sister, was a cube, each of its facets marked by black dots. After the Change two days ago, no one at first noticed that the Dark Circle's moons had changed into dice. They were too preoccupied with the fact that the Circle had torn into strips, those strips reforming into a kind of Moebius coil. That the Dark Land was magical had always been acknowledged in Ian's homeland of Mullshire; but this business was ridiculous. Who was it that said that God didn't throw dice?

And Mullshire! Mullshire had become a total wreck, magic spilling into it from the busted Circle like a flood through a cracked dam, spirits taking up residence in bodies live and dead, spreading havoc and chaos in their wake.

And it was all because Ian Farthing had been near Jat's Pass that fateful day that Princess Alandra had tried to escape. . . .

Ian thrust this guilty thought from his mind. Concentrate, he told himself as he moved along the makeshift path. Concentrate on getting back to the others, or you won't have the leisure to feel guilty, you'll just feel very dead!

His gnarled hairy fingers crept down carefully and touched the pommel of the Norx sword. The touch of the steel made him feel a little better, a little more secure. The thing was blasted heavy . . . but it was comforting to have it strapped to his side. He also carried the Pen that is Mightier Than the Sword in his pocket, but it was so unreliable he didn't trust it as a sole weapon. Like yesterday, when he thought he'd seen some creature stalking them and he'd pulled it out, all that happened was that he got ink all over his fingers! True, the creature turned out to be a harmless unicorn, but all the same it made Ian feel quite insecure. What, after all, if it had been a dangerous, vicious unicorn intent upon goring Ian Farthing with its sharp horn?

Still, whatever else it was, it had been a delicious unicorn.

Hillary had turned down the treat, but ravenous hunger had overcome any gustatory scruples on the parts of Ian and the six questing knights. Some kind of curse might accompany the killing of a unicorn, Hillary had mumbled after she'd gotten over her tears concerning Sir Mortimer's swift release of arrow into the thing's neck. Bloody well cursed enough, this place, the others had agreed. Any further curse would just get confused and lost.

Hillary . . . he had to get back to Hillary, certainly. Ian didn't like the thought at all of the fifteen-year-old alone so long with a bunch of men, be they chivalrous knights or no. Yes, this was the path, he thought as he recognized an oak that had apparently been struck by lightning. Split in twain, it still smelled of charred bark.

And were those voices stirring in the distance? He prayed that it was so. He—

To his left, a figure rose up from behind a bush. It growled.

Ian shrieked. His load of firewood flew up in the air, tumbling down willy-nilly, one bit striking him on the noggin. Ian reached for the short sword at his side as the figure stepped out before him on the pathway.

"Boo!" said the knight. "My goodness, Ian Farthing! Have a care! That's tonight's supply of heat and warmth for our weary bodies!" The man chuckled. "Still a joker to the last, though, my new companion," continued Sir Godfrey Pinkham. "Just a small jest on my part to keep you on your toes."

"Godfrey! I thought you were—"

"Now, now, settle yourself, my friend. Remember, I still have a difficult time understanding your quite garbled manner of speaking, though your speech seems to have cleared up considerably since that run-in you had with that noxious giant hand barring our path. We were just worried about you, my dear boy, and so I thought I'd take it upon myself to venture out into the darkness and make sure you were still in one piece. Now be a good lad and pick this wood back up again and follow me back. The chaps are tired of cold unicorn roast and would very much like to get a decent fire going so we can cook up something proper."

With that, the knight spun on his heel and began to saunter back.

"Wait, Godfrey," Ian called, desperately picking up the scattered pieces of wood. "Wait for me, please! I'm not sure of the path!"

"Bait? Yes, and bait you'll be for some fanga-morph or bandersnatch if you don't hurry along. Chop chop, Ian!"

Ian reassembled as much of the pile as he could before losing sight of Sir Godfrey; he dashed after him, dropping a piece or two of firewood in the process. By the time Ian caught up with the re-treating knight, they had both entered the clear-ing where the questing party made camp for the evening. Two knights poked a roaring fire while the other three seemed to be working at divesting themselves of their chain mail.

"Right, Ian," said Godfrey. "I thought that might encourage you to speed things up. You have much to learn, dear boy, about many things, and I shall do my very best to endeavor that you receive the best education possible. Who knows? Perhaps when things are put aright and we make it back to Mull, you might even qualify as my special lackey. I should like that, Ian. Always like to do my bit for the underdog, don't you know?"

"Thank you, sir," said Ian, actually feeling grate-ful only that he was back with the company.

Godfrey swiveled about, hand on hip. "I sin-cerely hope that was 'thank,' Master Snotface. If so, you really must work on your 'th' sounds."

"Ian!" a girl's voice cried. "Oh, Ian, I was so worried about you!" With a flow of long red tresses and a scrape of pants, Hillary Muffin ran from where she was brushing her horse to greet her friend.

"Right, Hiller," said Ian. "Would you give me a hand with this firewood? About to bust a gut, I am, an' no one else seems eager to help."

Hillary nodded and lifted off some of the heavy wood. Her blue eyes shone with happiness in the firelight as she looked at Ian. She was the only person who could actually understand what Ian Farthing pronounced through his mangled mouth. She had always understood, even when she was just a child. She was Ian's dearest and only true friend, but he almost wished now that she hadn't come along on this dangerous quest . . . and certainly he wished now that *he* hadn't, gorgeous princess or no gorgeous princess.

But then, they really had no choice if they wanted to put things aright back in Mullshire. No choice at all.

Sir Godfrey in the lead, they marched to the campfire. Godfrey pointed to the ground as he removed the hood of his capuchon, revealing his wealth of healthy blond curls. "Right there on this dry patch, if you please, my friends. Billy here seems to have appointed himself as this evening's keeper of the fire."

"Billy" was Sir William McIllvaine, a squat powerful older man who spoke little and dourly. His forecast concerning this quest was certain doom for them all, and every movement he made was part of some private march to the grave. Still, according to Sir Godfrey, there was no better companion to be had in the midst of a melee of swinging weapons, and thus the gloom could be accommodated. Now Sir William eyed the enlarged pile a moment, reached out stubby fingers, and felt the wood.

"Damp," he pronounced.

"Oh bother!" said Hillary tartly. "It will burn quite nicely. I felt that wood, and it was about the best we can expect in a place like this, so don't complain, especially after Ian went to all the trouble of getting it for you lazy oafs!"

"Madam, again you stretch the bounds of our chivalry," exclaimed Sir Mortimer Shieldson, through his droopy mustache but with precise diction. Sir Mortimer smiled, more than a trace of malice to his aspect. "But come, have a slice of unicorn meat and all is forgiven!"

Hillary blanched and turned away. "That poor darling innocent, and you had to butcher it. Didn't you see the look on its face? All it wanted was help—it was frightened, for its world had changed. But no—all you could think of was your big belly's rumblings! And you call yourself a gentleman."

"He was almost certainly also considering his purse," said Sir Godfrey, warming his hands by the fire. Light flickered over his handsome regular features, and for the thousandth time Ian Farthing envied him for that regular, smooth face. Ian's was swarthy and irregular, with bumps and lumps, ugly as his twisted body. Ian envied all of Sir Godfrey's firm, well-muscled frame. "I've heard tell that unicorn horns fetch a pretty penny if you find the right alchemist or sorcerer to sell them to. And don't try to deny it, Morty, you wicked scoundrel." The knight's green eyes gleamed as he smiled. "I saw you tuck that trophy in your saddlebag!"

"So what if I did!" Sir Mortimer said defensively. "I nailed the bloody beast, didn't I? And I skinned the thing and gutted it, and what happened? You gluttons finished most of it in barely a day. And for this you would conspire to deny me a bit of bone as trinket? Your ingratitude truly wounds this big heart of mine."

"Bah," said Sir Oscar Cornwall, scratching an

armpit after carefully placing his chain mail in a bag so that it would not rust. "Let him keep his horn, I say. I still have indigestion from that beast."

They were Mullshire's finest, these knights, stars of the Tournament Team, and Sir Godfrey had picked each one for abilities that had been proved —but, alas, only in mock battle. None had ever been on a quest before, and while they were all full of manly bravado, boasting of their talents and accomplishments, at unguarded moments Ian could see the flickers of anxiety in their eyes as they looked out upon the bleak contortions of this changing magical land.

Especially after what had happened to Sir Mallory, the lost seventh knight that Ian had replaced to form a numerologically sound grouping. They didn't talk about Sir Mallory much, but Ian gathered that his death in the jaws of a giant hand had been particularly grisly.

"Right!" said Sir Mortimer, pushing back his long dark hair and retying it into a ponytail behind his head. His ancestry was pure Anglo-Saxon, and it showed in the sharp shapings of his nose, cheekbones, and chin. "Don't begrudge a poor knight his paltry souvenirs, for God's sake! Besides, this business of a unicorn horn's having magical properties could be pure poppycock. I just like the way it looks!"

With his characteristic sneaky grin, Sir Godfrey gazed over to his saddlebags. "Well, there is one person who is quite knowledgeable in such matters. In fact, in this sort of thing he is quite a'head' of us all!" Godfrey snorted and slapped his leg. "What do you say, gents, shall we dig into our skulls together on this one?"

The assembled knights chuckled at that one,

but Ian could only shudder, not relishing the notion one jot.

"Here now, Pinkham, do you think it wise to bother Roth Kogar again today? God knows he needs his beauty sleep!" joked Sir Stephen Jentile, a neat, well-kempt knight now industriously polishing his sword.

Sir Godfrey waved away the notion. "Oh, he hasn't got anything else to do, what with the sleeping spell old Lord Morgsteen's put him under. Might as well give it a try and see if the Dark Lord is transmitting from his sorcerous manse this black hour." The young knight stepped over to the saddlebags by the tethered horses and began to untie a pouch that looked as if it held a bowling ball.

"Must I put up with this awful nonsense?" Hillary said, her hands knotted in fists as she glared at Sir Godfrey. She appeared about ready to bolt, so Ian grabbed her ankle before she could rise all the way. Hillary tumbled with an "Oof!"

"Where can you go to, Hiller?" Ian whispered. "Stay here, where you're safe."

"Safe with the likes of that . . . that thing?" Hillary said. "I just wish we didn't need it to guide us! I should like to throw it into some deep loch or bury it! It's even nastier than these knights of ours!"

"Shush, Hiller, and listen to what it says. Besides, don't you want to hear about what we can do with a unicorn horn?" Ian's interest picked up at the notion. "Why, it might help us to find Princess Alandra more quickly. We might even get out of this situation alive."

"You just want to be near that wretched princess, don't you, Ian Farthing? The way you talk about her you'd think she was an angel or something."

"Christ, Hiller, you're the one who wanted me to go. Would you make up your mind? Anyway, look . . . Godfrey's got the thing. Let's see if he can wake it up!"

Sure enough, Sir Godfrey Pinkham was carrying a roundish burden into the firelight. It was a severed head—a particularly large and brutish head with long black hair and thick imperious features. It was a head that Ian Farthing knew too well. After all, it was he who had cut it off in battle with the mechanical body of the Dark Lord Roth Kogar, with the help of the Pen Mightier Than the Sword, of course.

But that was a whole other story, and Ian didn't much like to dwell on its memory, since he'd nearly been killed that awful day!

Sir Godfrey threw the head to Sir Mortimer cheerily. "Well, if he doesn't light up, we can always play catch, what?"

His teeth on edge, Sir Mortimer, with a good deal more respect for the head than his leader showed, gingerly placed the head on a clump of grass. "Have a care, Pinkham. This chap is the best thing we have going for us!"

"Perhaps, perhaps," said Godfrey, drawing out his dagger as he knelt down before the bodiless head. He tapped the thing on its ear. "Calling all Dark Lords! Wake up, wake up, Roth Kogar." He displayed the gleaming blade. "We want to pick your brain!"

Suddenly, the head's mouth twitched. The wide nostrils of the long nose flared. And the eyelids opened, gleaming with a feral fire that was not a reflection of the stuff that chewed on the pile of wood at camp center.

"Dark . . . it's dark here," said Lord Roth Kogar in a voice deep and clear and sonorous. "Have you bumpkins gotten yourselves lost again?"

"No, Kogar, your directions seem to be quite sound, thank you," said Sir Godfrey, pacing in a manner he seemed to favor at lordly times, since it flapped his cape impressively and lent a certain drama to his words. "Actually, we were curious about something potentially magical, and since you are the deposed lord of an entire quadrant of this wretched and sorcerous place, we figured you to be our most likely authority on the subject."

The eyes in the head surveyed the knights within its view and then it smiled. "Happy to be of service, gentlemen."

"I'm not sure if we told you in our brief talk today," continued Sir Godfrey. "But Sir Mortimer killed a unicorn yestereve and has apparently saved the horn. We quite simply were wondering if unicorn horns are invested with any kind of magic, and if so, if that magic can be of benefit to our endeavor."

The dark fiery eyes flicked over to Sir Mortimer Shieldson. "A unicorn, eh? Oh, brave, brave fellow. Those are fearsome beasts, unicorns." His voice dripped sarcasm. "Quite rare in any other plane than this, and had you shot it elsewhere, I fear you'd have gotten into a great deal of trouble with the authorities, to say nothing of virgins. But then, the latter are almost as rare these immoral times, aren't they?"

"Didn't bring you up from slumber for that sort of lecture, old boy." Sir Godfrey deftly finished cleaning a thumbnail, then stuck his dagger back in its sheath.

"Right. Unicorns. Rather richly symbolic beasts in many cultures. Shall I rattle off a few bits of information on the subject for you?"

"No, Kogar. We just want to know about the horn."

"You ate the beast, though, eh? Never heard of that. Of course, you're still alive and nothing bad has happened yet—still, even I would have second thoughts about consuming unicorn flesh. Tempting the gods, you might say. In any event, yes, the horn is valuable. For instance, should you be poisoned, unicorn-horn powder is an excellent antidote. And alchemists adore the stuff— quicksilver to lionish sulfur. They can concoct all kinds of things. So I would suppose you could sell it. Hang onto it, though, through the quest, because you're quite right, you never know when you might have use for it."

"You see, I was quite right to save it," Sir Mortimer said, beaming.

"Just watch out for vengeful lions," teased Kogar. "As for curses . . . well, it's all mixed up now and I doubt if a curse will be able to find you through all this mess. Speaking of which, did you make much distance this day?"

"Not bad, but it exhausted our horses," replied Sir Godfrey. "We had to walk them the last bit."

"No problem. Transportation problems will be solved soon, I promise. You have seen the cliff formations I spoke of?"

"The axlike things. Yes, we passed them just after noon, though only two were left standing."

"Not surprising. This land was literally ripped

apart. Only because of its magical properties was everything not leveled."

"Have you heard any more, perhaps, about why this madness has occurred?" Hillary demanded.

"Ah, it is the brave young girl," said Kogar, gazing her way. "Constantly inquisitive. No, dear one. Do you not remember that my consciousness is imprisoned in my sleeping body? My sole means of transportation was the mechanical body which your friend Ian here deprived me of. My only remaining servants were killed, and only through a defeat of my archenemy Lord Snirk Morgsteen can my sleeping spell be annulled and my body released. No, Hillary Muffin, I know nothing, though I have a few random suspicions."

"Suspicions?" said Sir Godfrey. "You never spoke before of suspicions, Lord Kogar."

"You never bothered to ask, being far too literal-minded, Pinkham. Besides, I have had time to ponder the matter in these days that have passed since our brush with Apocalypse."

"We're all ears, Lord Kogar," Sir Godfrey said. "But does it change our plans at all?"

"No, no, absolutely not. I suspect that all this business with Princess Alandra is only a part of the problem. The balance of power is far askew in the Dark Land, and thus it has difficulty supporting the flux of energies from other universes. My belief is that the land has contorted into a shape that can accommodate this shifting in thaumaturgical powers. But for how long?"

"You mean there's a chance that everything could just . . ." Hillary gazed about fearfully. "Just crumble?"

"More than a chance, a certainty," said Kogar.

"The question is, will it occur next year, or next week?"

"And a successful rescue of Alandra will solve the problem?" Ian ventured hopefully.

"I think that is too much to ask for, but it will certainly be a decided start to reestablishment of an equilibrium."

Kogar's thoughts sounded too pat, too glib, to Ian. Why were they even asking the awful tyrant these questions? Had they forgotten that the Dark Lord most likely did nothing that was not ultimately in his own interest? His talk of reformation and change was simply too ridiculous. The man was simply stuck now in a situation in which he had no control. He had to manipulate those who held power over his mechanical head. Ian would have to remind the others of this once Lord Kogar had signed off for the evening.

"Just exactly what is so special about this Princess Alandra, anyway?" Hillary demanded. "How did she get to be so special?"

Lord Kogar sighed. "No one is really quite sure. She is the daughter of the late Leodegrance Bellworthy, Last of the Bright Lords, King of the Primary Quadrant. Legend has it that she was conceived of an angel, then bestowed upon the Bright Lord as a promised future queen who would unite the four quadrants into harmony. She is called the Key, and it is believed that this is because somehow she embodies a magical quality that, when mature, will meld together the contrasting and chaotic forces that churn about within the Dark Land and its very nature and form will alter. That she is magical anyone with the Sight or the Touch can immediately tell—but the nature of that magic is strikingly alien and fits no known pattern.

"In other words, Hillary Muffin, we shall simply have to wait and see. But meanwhile, you not so gentle knights have the task of getting to her alive, which I pray you will concentrate on as opposed to the hunting of unicorns. By that time, I suspect that by putting our heads together, we will have arrived at some sort of appropriate course of action, yes? Any further questions?"

The other knights, quite a bit more leery of the head than Ian, Hillary, and Godfrey, who had spoken with it more, shook their heads emphatically and grunted negatives.

"Very well then, perhaps we should not wear out our connection with too long an unnecessary chat."

Awareness winked from the eyes like extinguished lights.

"I had more questions I could have asked him!" Hillary said.

"Next time, Hiller," Ian promised. "Now let's see what we've collected to eat other than unicorn meat. You know, we're going to have to learn not to be quite so squeamish if we're going to survive."

While Ian and Hillary went to their shared pack to examine their supplies, the other men arranged themselves for their knight's rest, finding the most comfortable spots for their bedclothes, then preparing themselves for dinner. Their arrows that day had found their marks in two rabbits and several pheasants, so with what was left of the unicorn meat, they had quite a bit to eat.

"I hope you don't expect to eat it all, blast you!" Sir Godfrey said. "Save some for tomorrow. No telling how much we'll be able to forage or kill then! Precious little is my guess. We've just been lucky so far."

Ian and Hillary had found their supplies limited to the bread and cakes she'd stashed before she set out to help Ian and the apples and berries they'd managed to pluck along the way. Ian wondered if he shouldn't learn to shoot a longbow. Either that or get Hillary to ask the others for some of the rabbit when it was roasted. He'd been eating apples all day, and was developing a terrible case of gas.

"No!" she answered promptly. "I'll do nothing of the sort, Ian . . . at least not today, after our discussion concerning the unicorn meat. They'd just laugh at me, and I'd rather endure bread and apples than their laughter. In a day or two, they'll be tired enough and forgetful enough of my anger, and I'll ask then. But go ahead and beg if you want to. You're pretty good at it, even if they have a hard time understanding you."

"Oh, thanks so much, Hillary Muffin! I've never begged, I've asked nicely for things. I've worked for my living all my life, but Da never gave me much in the way of wages, you know that. And wait a moment—when you were younger, you were glad of the occasional sweetmeat or fruit or drink I received free from the odd villager who actually felt sorry for this state I'm in."

"Too true, Ian," she said, regarding his bent face, his contorted fingers. "I'm sorry." She leaned over and kissed his forehead, her hand brushing the back of his neck, touching the two large pimplelike bumps that he hid beneath his hair. "Yow!" she said and moved her hand away. She felt his forehead, then reached back again. "You don't seem to have a fever, but your neck bumps

. . . they're quite warm. Did you know that, Ian?"

Ian nodded. "Yes. They have been ever since I fought that creature barring our way and entered the Dark Circle."

"Do you think it has something to do with that story Jacob Tillster told—about seeing you as a child falling from that rent in the sky? Too bad he got knocked out, or he might have seen more."

"Aye, Hiller, it would fit, wouldn't it? I mean, what with me found wanderin' the streets without a memory, and taken in by the Farthings, which they do confess to. But what the hell it has to do with these bumps, I just don't know." Ian felt himself shudder with discomfort. "An' I'd just as soon not talk about it."

"But Ian . . . you're getting better!" remarked Hillary cheerfully. "You've straightened a bit, your complexion is clearer . . . and you now speak a little more like usual folk." Her eyes shone as she stroked him gently on the back. "Let me tell you what I think. It's what I've always felt deep down but couldn't quite explain." She smoothed the wrinkles in her breeches, cupped her hands daintily in her lap, and held her head up very straight, as though making some kind of royal pronouncement. "I think that you're from someplace else, someplace very grand, with bright shiny people all about, good people, who are at the center of all that is right about existence. Somehow you got lost, or were stolen, or something quite sad, and something went quite wrong and you ended up in Mullshire. Now being so very far from the source of life and energy, your poor body was very hurt and became—not normal. But the closer you get to your home—and you are going to your home, I just feel it in my bones, Ian!—the closer you come to this wonderful mystical place, the straighter will be your back, the more even your legs, the more beautiful your face. Not that I find them wrong now, Ian, just different—but you've never liked them much, have you?"

"Zounds, no! I'm a laughingstock!"

"Not anymore, Ian. And get that thought out of your head this instant!" She slapped him upside the head, and Ian yelped. "There. I've helped it. No more of this self-deprecation manure, do you hear me? To me, you're a prince in peasant's rags, and that's what you are to other people as well, do you understand?" She shook a scolding finger under his nose.

Ian had to chuckle ruefully. "You mean like Lazlo the Wandering Angel."

"Yes, that's just what I mean!" Her pert up-turned nose tilted upward farther, as though she were a princess in peasant's clothing. "And don't you ever forget it, or I'll smack you again!"

"Yes, Hillary," he said, automatically cringing away from the threat. He could smell the rabbit flesh at the fire, and his stomach churned with hunger. "I think I'll just go over and make a princely request for a piece of meat. All right?"

Hillary, her nose twitching uncomfortably with the delicious smell now mingling with the raw damp of forest scent, let her eyes drift for a second, then firmly brought them back and folded her arms together with resolve. "Do what you like, Ian, but don't ask for any more of my apples this night if you choose to munch on rabbit, tainted, no doubt, by unicorn blood!"

Not responding, Ian rose as gracefully as he could, tripping and staggering only once in the process, and made his way over to where Sir

Oscar was just putting the finishing sizzles to the pair of carcasses spitted on a stick. Cornwall was the second-youngest of the knights. He wore no facial hair, he kept his hair short and neat, and he was particularly lithe and agile; Ian had seen him in action upon the gaming fields. His brown eyes were open and nonjudging. From what Ian could tell, he was the best-natured of this entire lot, and he hoped he could strike up some kind of friendship with Cornwall.

"Hello, there, Sir Oscar," Ian said, unwrapping his worn cloak a bit now that he was closer to the fire.

"Hail and well met, Ian Farthing," answered the knight in a much softer tone than the usual ringing tones employed by his more image-conscious companions. Ian was also particularly impressed with the fine clothes that Sir Oscar wore. Finely cut dark woolen breeches, shiny boots, a bright red silk blouse beneath a thick jerkin, and a fur cape—his family must be very wealthy to provide such nice apparel for their son. Sir Oscar took the feather-topped woodsman's cap he affected from atop his head and bowed cordially. "And how may I be of service?"

"Well, I was rather hoping," returned Ian, "that I might have a morsel from one of those rabbits." He motioned toward the others, who seemed busy consuming the sweeter-tasting pheasants. "There doesn't seem to be much call for them, and—"

A perplexed look filled Sir Oscar's face. "I'm sorry, old chap, I can't quite make out what—" Then a grin appeared. "Oh, quite! You'd like a bit of this rabbit! Well, of course! It's for us all—you don't really have to ask!" He reached up and patted Ian familiarly on the back. "You're an interesting addition to a questing party, Ian. And a valuable one, so let's not hear any balking at asking for a simple rabbit's leg to fill your belly. And why don't you take one for that pretty girlfriend of yours, too?" He winked over at Hillary, who apparently had been watching the proceedings, since she swung her head back around huffily.

The attention toward Hillary made Ian feel peculiarly disturbed. But his predominant feeling at that moment was hunger. So when Sir Oscar withdrew the rabbits from the flame and waved them in the night air a bit to cool them down, he found his stomach gurgling with anticipation and his hand reaching out.

"Thanks very much, Sir Oscar," he said, "and please, if you'd like some apples, we've got—"

A hand grabbed him from behind and pulled him back.

"No grub for Master Farthing right now, Sir Oscar," said Sir Geoffrey Pinkham somberly. "He's got a task to do, first."

"But Pinkham, he bloody well brought us that pile of firewood!" Sir Oscar objected, rising up, face coloring a bit. "Have a heart, man!"

"My heart is right where it belongs, Cornwall ... with the group," said Sir Godfrey sternly. "I've only just noticed that the pile is considerably depleted from its state when you were lugging it in, Farthing. You must not have picked up all the pieces you dropped, eh? What we have now won't get us through the night."

"Well then, why don't you or I go out there?" said Cornwall.

"Steady on, Oscar. Let me have a brief word with Master Farthing. You forget that Ian and I have known each other for years. We're the best

of friends, and Ian takes my advice, right, Ian?"
Godfrey punched Ian in the shoulder in a fashion
filled with manly bonhomie.

"Actually, Godfrey, if you want to know the
truth—" began Ian, but he was interrupted by a
bear hug from Sir Godfrey.

"You see what I mean, Oscar. There's a good lad,
Ian, now let's wander a few paces and have a chat."

Flummoxed, Ian could not object.

"There now. I just want to say, Ian, that I stand
by you all the way. This quest would not be
possible but for you, and personally I intend it to
be a mission filled with stout-hearted glory. But I
am the leader, Ian," Godfrey intoned deeply, shaking his finger to underscore his words, "and I
need the support of all my men, especially you.
How will the others look up to me if you don't?
And you can show your respect by simply going
and picking up that wood you dropped, no objections given, understood?"

"But Godfrey, it's dark!"

"Excellent—I'm glad you agree." Godfrey
marched him back beside the campfire. "I knew you
were the bravest of us all. So go and fetch that
wood and you will have a nice bit of rabbit waiting for you, Ian Farthing."

"For God's sake, at least let him have one of the
torches!" Sir Oscar said.

"And why not? Sir Ronald! You're closest to
the appropriate bags. Bring us one of those smaller
torches with a touch of paraffin to it!"

Sir Ronald Komquatte wiped pheasant grease
off on his trousers and got the torch quickly. Sir
Godfrey lit it in the campfire and presented the
modest flame-on-a-stick to Ian as though it were a
gift. "Any other bit of wood you see, we'll be glad

of, Ian, and just remember, if you don't get enough you'll just have to go out in the middle of the night, so do a good job."

"I'd best go with him, Godfrey," insisted Sir Oscar.

"Don't worry, Oscar, 'e'll be all right. 'E's magical!" cried one of the knights, and they all laughed.

Ian would very much have liked company, but Godfrey did make a kind of sense. "Thank you, Sir Oscar, but it's very close and it won't take long." Cornwall seemed to understand the shaking of the head more than the words. He just shrugged and sat back down to take care of the toasting rabbit.

"I shan't be long," he said, striking off for the path he had only recently trod.

"Just think 'shake of a rabbit's tail,' Ian Farthing!" cried one of the knights, and bellowing laughter followed his heels.

He didn't even look at Hillary as he left, nor did she try to stop him. Was she mad at him? Just sulking, most like.

Well, onward, onward into the unknown, he told himself, bracing against the chill as he rambled past the crooked trees, his nostrils awake again to the mold and the dead leaves and pine scents. I shall show them once more that I am no coward. . . .

And perhaps, he thought, I might just convince myself!

At least he still had the Norx sword strapped to his side, comforting if heavy. The sword, of course, was the relic of his initial confrontation with Alandra and her fearsome captors . . . the business that had started all this fantastic odyssey. If only somehow he could turn back time, and prevent his terrible mistake. Princess Alandra might have made it in her mad dash atop her horse, Crackers, reached her savior, Sir Godfrey—and none of this insanity would have occurred. He would be tucked safely and warmly back home after a day's cobbling, sipping a warm toddy, and the world wouldn't look like some weird pretzel!

Godfrey was right. He did owe the man obedience. Ian certainly couldn't make the journey alone, and it was Godfrey, not Ian, who struck out immediately to rescue Alandra. No, Ian had run away, frightened out of his wits.

Right. They had to stick together as a group. Groups had to have leaders. And Sir Godfrey was their leader, and must be obeyed, even if he was a bit of a rotter, as Hillary pointed out. At least he treated Ian with much more respect than he used to.

Still, it was wise to be careful with the fellow, at least in small matters. He was surely still capable of practical jokes. It was simply in Godfrey's nature, and always had been, ever since they'd been children.

The place where Ian had been surprised and lost his hold upon the firewood was just beyond a dip in the ground. A bit of a bower, thought Ian to himself, gazing into the darkness filled with wind sounds. What little people have capered here, full of mischief? What pixies or brownies, leprechauns or kobolds or other magical beings, have passed through this place?

And what monsters?

Ian, of course, knew all about monsters. His mum and da would always delight in telling him about the creatures they had heard lived in the Dark Circle, creatures who would, from time to

time, venture out and devour bad boys. He still
had difficulty going near rivers and streams for
fear that Peg Prowler and Jenny Greenteeth might
drag him in and drown him, snagging him with
their long claws and floating seaweed hair.

Yes, the bogies and bogles that Ian had run
from in his night- and day-mares had been numer-
ous—

And now he walked by night in a land where
they most likely truly existed.

Ian tried to whistle in the dark, failing miserably.

He found the firewood by tripping over one of
the short branches. Sure enough, there was plenty
left, scattered all about the sides of the trail. Godfrey had been quite right. Ian had been in such a
hurry to get back to the campsite that he had
neglected his duty of hauling back the full load.

The torch had been whittled down to a sharp
edge. Ian stuck it in the moist topsoil and commenced collecting the wood as quickly as his
quirky limbs would allow. Hillary had been speaking truth, though; he had changed. He was more
limber now, and his club foot seemed not quite
so awkward. Perhaps soon he would even have to
readjust his special shoe, he thought happily. Well,
no problem with that—after all, he was a cobbler.

He put the last bit of wood in the pile, and he
was bending awkwardly to pick up the torch when
the sound started.

It was a mewling squeak, accompanied by much
rattling of bushes, and it startled Ian just enough
to cause him to lose his grasp on the firewood.

This time, though, he wasn't frightened so much
as he was angry. He was so angry, in fact, that he
forgot it was dark and dangerous and nearly lost
his senses.

"Damn your eyes, Godfrey, I'm trying to do my best, but if you persist in your hounding and pranks . . ."

He shocked himself by the vehemence of his anger. He was never like this! Still, he was swept along in its flow. He picked up the torch, drew his Norx sword from its sheath, and slashed off the tops of two bushes.

"Do you hear me?" he said, the fire lessening somewhat, a squiggle of doubt entering his mind. "Pinkham, show yourself! No doubt the others are there as well, having a laugh on me! Now come out and apologize!"

He lifted the torch higher to get a better look. The thrashing continued, and it was coming toward him.

Only it didn't sound like the mashing of boots against dead leaves, it sounded like something much bigger, much heavier.

Good God, thought Ian. Whatever have I gotten myself into here? Fear seemed to freeze him into place.

This couldn't be Godfrey . . .

. . . and therefore . . .

The creature bashed back two well-leafed saplings with paws that bore claws curved like scimitars and were not much smaller than well-sized scimitars at that.

The light from Ian's torch guttered over twisted rags covering a greenish body below a face that was about as ugly as ugly got while trying to maintain a semblance of creaturehood.

"Uhh, I really d-didn't m-mean to c-call you names," said Ian Farthing.

He tried to remember how to run.

chapter two

the four-sided die glittered in candlelight as it fell to the table. It bounced once, twice, and then began spinning like a top on one of its vertices.

Swallowing back his impatience, Crowley Nilrem, Gaming Magus, waited as the Die of Dances did its pirouette to the music of his breathing. He hoped against hope that it would come up a four. If it was a four, it would be for the fourth time, and the ancient magic device of chance would be only three more rolls away from the effect that was needed, the effect that Jason Dunworthy, dead now, had not had life enough to intone after Nilrem had cut him down from the ceiling.

The crystalline die swirled, and had it not been for Crowley Nilrem's own power, it might have hypnotized its thrower with the splintered light it cast.

Like a whirling dervish it spun. Nilrem concentrated with all his might, though control of the casting of magical dice was not his strong suit.

Damn, if only Rambonthius Rickshaw were here! In a former life, that magus had worked the tables at a magical gambling hall, and could load or

throw dice better than anyone. If not for his es-
sentially low-grade abilities in other magi matters, he might have been foremost among the Nine.
Where were the others, anyway? Had they not felt
his summons? Had the catastrophe been that great?
Perhaps they had all ended up like Dunworthy,
forced to imitate the hanged man of the Tarot
pack by the returned Rawlings, some sacred die
like this spinning one piercing their temples.

Whatever the situation, Crowley Nilrem thought,
stroking a long, disheveled sideburn, it was going
to be a damned dicey one. Damned dicey.

Two things then occurred at once.

The doorbell rang.

The die clicked to a halt, coming to rest on its
four-dotted side for the fifth time in a row.

It was the first time either thing had happened
in the hours that had passed since Nilrem had
entered Dunworthy's mansion.

Excellent! Only two more successful rolls to
go, and he could entreat help from the others. A
small chink of light thus breaking through the
thunderclouds in his mind, he stood and, in standing, caught sight of himself in an oval mirror with
a gilt baroque frame.

Gadzooks! What a mess! Crowley Nilrem's
Victorian-style dress was usually immaculate, his
cuffs starched, his pants neatly pressed. His grooming he kept equally sharp, down to the quite
delicate and difficult spells he had perfected to
maintain his manicure and pedicure.

But now! Now he looked like an unraveling
ball of twine! His hair was a floppy mass of disor-
ganized curls, his elbows stuck through his top-
coat, his sleeves were frazzled and dripping
threads. All the buttons had popped off his tweed

waistcoat, releasing his cherished Joinville tie to flap like a stringy flag attacked by some army of cats.

He would be a laughingstock before the others. How those Gaming Magi would chuckle to see their vain colleague such a wretched ragbag! The Gaming Magi were variously enemies and allies as they tugged and plotted for power through strategy, magic, diplomacy, and chance. Their relationships were invariably of the love/hate variety, but most recently the balance had turned more toward suspicion and backbiting than any of the kindlier attitudes. What a time for this wretched business to happen! What a time for a previously enjoyable, if occasionally deadly, series of power trips to be so confoundedly tripped up!

Hastily, Crowley Nilrem did his best to at least repair his hair, at first muttering a spell, and when that failed, wetting his fingers and using them for a comb.

Dammit, what a bother, he thought, stamping his feet as the doorbell rang again. "Coming!" he called, scuffing along, the soles of his previously shiny Oxfords flapping as he walked. "Keep your pants on!"

He'd neglected to put an end tag on his hair-fix spell; what remained of the magic that held his threads patchily together misunderstood, and his suspenders unsnapped, allowing his breeches to slip down to his ankles.

He tripped, his fall only slightly cushioned by a richly patterned rug, scattering his hair in disarray again.

"Dammit!" he cried, struggling to his feet and pulling his trousers back up again just as the doorbell rang and a voice cried, "We know you're in there, Nilrem, and we certainly would like to have a few choice words with you!"

"Coming!" called Crowley Nilrem, limping along through a particularly large chamber, decorated in Jason Dunworthy's favored Art Deco style, all curlicues and peacock feathers in vases and pots, tastefully spaced furniture and Greek scrolled columns and archways. "I'm here! Please don't go away, chaps. Please!"

His dignity be damned, this was a dire situation.

Finally, he reached the door, unlocked the latch, and pulled the heavy oaken thing open.

Beyond shone a horizon of stars, random comets attempting the occasional connect-a-dot spree. Ground fog curled up along the edge of the front lawn like wraiths in a slow-motion discotheque. A frigid blast of air touched Crowley Nilrem like an ice giant's smooch.

On the porch stood the remaining seven Gaming Magi in assorted curious poses.

Crowley Nilrem blinked as the magi moved into the light spilling from the hallway.

"Oh my goodness," said Nilrem, losing his clutch on the top of his trousers. They fell to his shoes.

"Yes, Crowley Nilrem," said the alligator in aviator goggles. "An apt comment. Things are getting out of hand!"

"What do you think you're staring at, Crowley Nilrem?" said the bulldog, pulling his cigar from his mouth as he accepted the stiff drink of scotch his fellow magus had just poured. "You don't look so wonderful yourself."

"Sorry, old man, but it just seems so . . ." Nilrem

poured himself a healthy dollop of the Highland dew. "Well, so—"

"Go ahead and spit it out," said Nostril Daymoos, who had grown a horse's head. "Appropriate! Well, Crowley, all I can say to that is, had you changed, there's no doubt you'd be a whole ass."

"Or maybe just the other way around!" honked Irler Mothwing, who had turned into a creature of the goosely persuasion, feathers and all; however, he still sported his characteristic polka-dot bow tie.

"Right, Nilrem," barked Barnum Armbruster, the upright bulldog in trousers. "We've answered your summons, but we would have come looking for you anyway. Just what in Hell's name is going on? Did someone change the Master Game to Animal Farm?"

They all stood or sat in Jason Dunworthy's study now, finally collected together for better or worse. Crowley Nilrem nervously checked the hold his suspenders had on his trousers, adjusted his jacket, and surveyed his audience, trying to remember what they used to look like, yet failing.

Here was Rambonthius Rickshaw, for instance, whiz wizard of the dice, parading about with the head of an alligator perched above his lapels. The original Rickshaw, of course, always wore aviator glasses on visiting days—but never before a four-foot-long tail sprouting from his rear end! And there was Igward T. LePouf, wearing his usual opera cape, cummerbund, and gloves—but on a body that looked half man and half elephant. But the truly astonishing new magi look belonged to Salvatore Amore, who had assumed the body of a pig, still keeping his quite tacky tux and tails, splattered with tomato sauce. Sally, as his friends called him, seemed to be rather enjoying his new character, parading like a newly crowned prince before a floor-length looking glass.

"Quite correct, dear boy," said the walrus-shaped Elwood Spiffington. "As I last recall, you had established a power enclave of Mothwing, Daymoos, and yours truly to help perpetrate the escape of Princess Alandra from Snirk Morgsteen and company, controlled by LePouf and Armbruster these turn-cycles—"

"No longer, mates!" objected Armbruster in his usual blustery fashion. "Haven't had a jot of influence over the dastard since all this brouhaha commenced. Lost control of me consciousness, though, I did, and woke up with me Wraith Board floatin' like an Escher nightmare and me lookin' like Winston Churchill with a hangover!"

"Nor have I," sniffed LePouf, pulling an elegant snuffbox from a pocket. "In fact, with the present chaos, it seems that none of us exercises any control upon his board. Our characters appear to have been either totally invested with free will, or influenced by some other outside forces! By the way, I neglected to ask . . . where is dear Jason? Turned into a rat and run away, I daresay."

"All in good time, LePouf," said Nilrem. "But you are quite right concerning the outside influence. In fact, I spoke to him. It's Colin. I'm afraid he's returned, and as you might expect he's not terribly happy with us."

LePouf, in the act of taking a pinch of snuff, suffered an explosive attack of the shakes, which spewed the fine tobacco dust up in a cloud. "Oh, Christ! Rawlings!" He sneezed violently through his abbreviated elephant trunk. "I had hoped that this was some sort of practical joke p-p-perpetrated

by you and Dunworthy, Nilrem! R-R-Rawlings
indeed!"

Crowley Nilrem gazed around with satisfaction
at the various degrees of shock registering in the
still quite human eyes of his refurbished col-
leagues. Thus his own eyes must have looked
clouded and stricken with alarm, as realization
had dawned upon him in stages.

Within moments, decanters tilted and tumblers
clanked as large dollops of alcohol were poured
and hastily polished off.

"Caesar returned from the grave," said Irler
Mothwing, amber drink dribbling from his beak.

"With an angry Jove at his elbow, hurling thun-
derbolts," continued Rambonthius Rickshaw, finally taking off his aviator goggles, fogged up
now.

"But I thought the bloody nails were fast in
his bloody coffin!" groaned Barnum Armbruster,
chewing nervously on his cigar. "I mean, there
were nine of us, and only one of him! We had
an airtight sorcerous conspiracy to rival the power
of the Lost Gamegod himself, praised be his
Name."

"Colin Rawlings," said Nostril Daymoos mus-
ingly as he shook his mane and snorted. "Why,
it's been centuries since the Exile Dispersion. . . ."

Elwood Spiffington waddled over to the drink
cabinet to look for some strong corn liquor.
"Though it would explain the chaos. That Rawlings
adored chaos—he's the one who perpetrated the
Circle to begin with, to say nothing of the game
rules we've been trying to alter for years."

"I just remembered," cried Rickshaw, his sharp
and crooked teeth clacking together in his excitement. "The last thing he said to us was, 'You

animals will hear from me again.'" He turned to Nilrem so quickly his tail whipped Damus in the leg. "So, Crowley. Tell us!"

Crowley Nilrem sipped his scotch pensively, letting its vapors loosen up his mind and his tongue. He gazed about at the motley assembly a moment, and suddenly realized that beneath the usual sorcerous scents, the booze, the cigar smoke, and the snuff, it was beginning to smell like a barnyard. He shook his head, wondering why he had been spared and what animal he would have turned into had he been affected by this part of this wide-ranging spell. Then he turned to his companions.

"It all started with my poor cat, Alabaster," he said, sitting down wearily at the glossily waxed walnut table and staring down at the Die of Dances. "And it's all the way up this far."

Apparently, it was the first time that any of them had noticed the die on the table. Several of the magi stepped back in fear and awe, while the others controlled their surprise only slightly better with coughs and blinks and honks or neighs. That die, after all, was what had turned the trick on Rawlings. Brutus's dagger. The stone on the grave. The stake in the heart. Its presence was physical evidence that Colin Rawlings, the Master himself, was very much active indeed upon the planes of existence intersecting in the Dark Circle.

No one spoke. They turned to Crowley Nilrem, waiting for the rest of the bad news.

"As you pointed out before, I was overseeing the crucial roll to determine the degree of success of Princess Alandra's flight from the castle of Snirk Morgsteen. I say this because not only had I per-

fected a particular control of my gaming dice
in this particular throw, but with the aid of my
allies, I had virtually assured that three-quarters
of the variations possible would spell sufficient,
if varied types of, success. Alas, when it came
time for the toss, my cat, Alabaster, whom you've
all met at one time or another, came bounding in
chasing a ghost-mouse. He knocked over a cande-
labra, my jacket and hair caught aflame, and I
threw the dice the wrong way, resulting in snake
eyes, the single throw that would spell disaster."

"And naturally you dealt with the cat, and the
bad vibrations inherent in it?" asked LePouf.

"Well, I had to! The positive sorcery I'd established, unreleased, began to shake and corrode
my entire mansion. I found poor Alabaster and
exiled him by tossing him down the Stellar Corridor into the Dark Circls, where he would be
neutralized.

"But the disintegration of my precious home
did not halt. And worse, when I returned to the
board, its symbolic pieces, scattered before, had
reassembled themselves in different positions. The
Norx had recaptured Alandra, Kogar had somehow been released, there was a new piece on the
board—well, I assume these changes were reflected
in the Wraith Boards in your respective domiciles."

As one, the other Gaming Magi nodded.

His throat dry at the memory, Crowley Nilrem
helped himself to another gulp of scotch. He proceeded to go into detail concerning the new setup
of the representative board pieces and what it
meant in the overall framework of the game.

"Of course, you all realize, in the light of the
events I describe what it will mean if Morgsteen
and his silly demimagicians, without being under

our control, get hold of Alandra again and figure out exactly why she is called the Key." He scowled. "Our fun and games of power have gotten out of hand, and our very existences are threatened."

"Yes, yes, we've figured that out by now, Crowley. Carry on with the story!" demanded Nostril Daymoos.

Nilrem took a deep breath and detailed how, still not realizing the true source of his problems, he had sought out the aid of his former Gameselves in a ritualistic ceremony. Colin Rawlings had disguised himself as a cowled monk and announced his presence at the meeting by killing the other Gameselves from the warrior to the dwarf, dispatching them with astonishing ease.

And then he issued a demand.

"He told me to call a meeting to order and be ready for his arrival. He told me that we would divine what he needed, and would make provisions. He acted as though we had already surrendered."

"Arrogant buffoon!" cried Amore with a porcine snort. "The game has not yet begun!"

"But look what he has done to us already!" cried Spiffington, worrying his whiskers. "He's always had more power than we have! We were just lucky and tricked him before."

"The interesting thing about him was that though he was most definitely Rawlings—I mean, there is no one else who has his aura—he was not yet corporeal. He was still starstuff, slowly collecting. Not at all fleshy—quite a sight."

"Perhaps that's what he wants—a new body," suggested Mothwing thoughtfully.

"Well, he shan't have one," squealed Spiffington.

"We shall fight him! So continue please, Nilrem. Why did you choose to come here?"

"Most centrally located, and Dunworthy was the most amiable of us all. I thought that if any of you had objections to a meeting, Dunworthy might be able to convince you otherwise. My mother suggested that. She's quite wise, you know."

"Your mother! Must you bring her into this?" said Rickshaw. "You know what happened last time."

"Quite, but for the sake of congeniality," retorted Nilrem, "I suggest we leave my dear mother out of this for now." Nilrem harrumphed. "Yes. I came here via Tarot Express Card to seek Jason Dunworthy's aid in summoning you all and making you all fully cognizant of our plight. I take it that at about the same time the Wraith Boards were changing, so were your appearances."

As one the group nodded.

"Yes. Well, I found poor Dunworthy strung up by his ankle like the hanged man, the Dance of Dies embedded in his temple. I cut him down, and just before he coiled off the old shuff, he told me that a roll of four seven times on the Die of Dances would—well, presumably, help; he died before he could explain. So I summoned you, and here we are, and there is poor Dunworthy yonder under that dropcloth, and here is the Die of Dances lying on its fifth four, with only two more fours to go." He turned to the alligator. "Rickshaw, you have a way with any dice. Would you care to exert your influence as I throw?"

"Here, wait a minute!" cried Armbruster, stepping doggedly forward. "How do we know the result is going to be desirable?"

"It seems to be what Dunworthy thought desirable," retorted Nilrem. "Have you any other suggestions? Or perhaps you're ready to just throw in the towel again to that crazy man Rawlings!"

"Hell no!" said Armbruster, retreating, his big pug face still stuck out. "I don't want to work for Rawlings again. I just ain't cut out for apprenticing no more. But what I'm saying is that I just don't want to go off half bloody cocked here! Let's work this out!"

Nilrem tossed a glance around the animal assembly, challenging. "Surely you all remember what that was like? Our games tied to the mercurial whims of a madman reinventing the concepts of good and evil, and often as not practicing the latter wholeheartedly. Or perhaps you'd like to undergo one of those delightful cosmic tea parties, eh? You could keep the Doormouse and March Hare such good company in your present guises." He paused for a dramatic silence, allowing his gaze to drift to each of the magi. "We have a democratic process in the Games now, gentlemen. Before, we suffered a tyrant. We have equality now; before we were fancy-panted slaves. We perform a vital function in the universes, our Games weave the threads of Fate for billions upon billions of creatures, and yet our games are fair because they are a balance of competition and chance, justice and chaos, intelligence and power. And what have we asked in return? Merely the pleasure and satisfaction of playing our roles unmolested by domination. This balance, this equilibrium, is coming apart now, and I suggest we forget our differences, dissolve our rivalries, ignore our puny separate needs, and commence to grapple with our ancient foe instead of kissing his feet once more. I shudder to think of the plans

Colin Rawlings has for a new multiuniversal reality-scaping. We have struggled so long to master the absurdities of his last endeavors! Yet you and I must face the fact that high among his priorities must be revenge upon us for his discorporation and exile. We cannot afford to express the fear we all feel, but must band our talents and energies together to influence the course of destiny within the altered Dark Circle in such a way as to restore our full powers and rid the multiuniverses once and for all of this cosmic ruffian!"

Crowley Nilrem cleared his throat and walked across the Persian carpet to the table holding the Die of Dances. The eyes of the others in their respective new faces followed him and watched as he picked up the die and held it out for all to observe, cradled in his palm.

A flash of lightning from the moil of clouds beyond the side windows momentarily heightened the shadows of this frieze. The room was suddenly cold, and the magi shuddered as one. Ropes of incense began to drift up from ornate silverworked burners hanging near the walls; the scent of sandalwood gently pervaded the air.

"Now, my fellow magi, if you will shut all other thoughts from your mind save for the image of four dots stamped upon this die, and concentrate, I shall attempt the casting of the sixth roll!"

Feathers ruffled. A tail wagged. Jaws snapped. Nostrils snorted. And then silence descended again as the members of the gathering concentrated.

Crowley Nilrem said a prayer to the Unknown, and he then cast the die.

It seemed to fall from his palm in slowed motion, catching the candlelights in its crystal guts and spinning them out like rays from some stylized sun. The die hit the table, bounced once, twice, and then settled firmly, four side triumphant.

Gasps of relief filled in the silence.

"Excellent, brethren," said Crowley Nilrem. "I sense your cooperation and concentration. Before the die spun and twirled and danced for a very long time. We have not lost our collective powers after all. Perhaps we do have more than just a thin chance against Rawlings."

"Doing my best," said Rambonthius Rickshaw, "but the field about that die—I haven't felt that confluence of powers in a very long time."

"Right, gentlemen," said Crowley Nilrem. "Take a few deep breaths, relax, and then again reach out with your minds and touch this die. If we can make it fall on the four once more, then we might enjoy the hope that our dear departed colleague hinted at before he died."

Again, as he concentrated, Nilrem felt an increased perception from all senses. Taste as the anticipation of success; smell as the mingled olfactory memories of Jason Dunworthy; touch as the prickles of pain past, pain future; hearing as all the possibilities sneaking around silence; sight as the mire of light and shadow beginning to quiver about him; and his further occult senses, a gentle clamor of unknown forces struggling for birth. Never before had such a feeling swept him up before casting. With confidence and grace, he flicked his hand, allowing the Die of Dances to depart into the clutches of gravity, kissing its flight with the mental image of a square of dots and the mental intonation of "Four! Four! Four!"

As though attracted by a magnet, the die dropped.

With no hesitation whatsoever, it spun into position, and landed directly on one side. It did not bounce, it did not even quiver uncertainly in place. It landed securely and firmly . . .

. . . on the number four.

Breaths released as the menagerie of magi relaxed and exchanged relieved glances. Crowley Nilrem could not take his eyes from the die, waiting to see what would happen.

The crystal Die of Dances began to pulse like a demented rainbow. As though forgetful of gravity, it lifted up into the air and began to shed shafts of colored light from all four facets as it ascended toward the ceiling. Halfway there, it halted and began to grow.

The magi backed away, shielding their eyes from the lights.

As the die grew, it began to spin slowly, imitating exactly the speed of the Wraith Board.

A ray of particularly intense light reached out and touched the covered body lying prone on the floor.

The dropcloth stirred. The body below it jerked once, then turned over and lifted itself up groggily.

Blinking in the light, Jason Dunworthy stared at his fellow Gaming Magi. Crowley Nilrem noted immediately that the hole in his forehead had healed completely.

"Hallo, chaps," said the resurrected Magus. "Come for a gamble or a gambol?" He looked more closely at the assembly. "I say, is it All Hallows' Eve? Or am I suffering from a particularly amusing dream?"

"Rawlings is back, Jason," said Nilrem, recovering from his surprise. "Don't you remember?"

Jason Dunworthy touched his forehead thought-fully, then said, "Oh my, yes. We're in a spot of trouble, aren't we?"

"Damned straight," said the Die of Dances, twirling gently. "You boys in a heap o' trouble, and I ain't just whistlin' Pixie!"

"I just remembered," said Crowley Nilrem, "why I never cared for that die very much."

chapter three

Ian Farthing stood staring at the thing in the bushes, not knowing whether to run or merely expire straight away from fright.

The creature was fully illuminated by the flickering light from his torch. It cringed before him as though it expected to be struck, even though it was at least a foot taller than Ian and much broader.

"Oh! Don't kill a poor sad and abandoned lady!" it said, its voice not much different from the sound of cats in conflict. "Please, I beg of you, good sir. Mercy, mercy, in the name of all that's holy."

At first glance, it seemed just a bundle of rags poorly stitched together, topped by a ruined mop. But upon closer inspection, a pair of bent and beclawed, twitching and snapping hands stuck out from the front, flesh the same green as the nose that poked from the mop strands of hair.

Ian, recovering, drew his Norx sword and cried, "Stand back, monster!"

Saucer eyes suddenly opened wide amid the straggly hair. Watery reflections of the torchlight bounced back a look of pure fear, and then the creature dived for the ground, whimpering and groveling. "Don't kill me, kind sir!" The thing shook like a wet dog as it attempted to kiss Ian's shoes. "Oh, please don't slash and mash these poor bones! I am so weary and hungry, and I saw a fire and these quivery nostrils smelled some food, and I thought I might beg—"

"Slash? Mash?" said Ian. "I'm not going to kill you, I thought you were going to kill me!"

The notion seemed to stun the creature. It peered up from its tangle of hair, purple eyes amazed. "Harmless Alison, kill? Oh, noble sir, dispel that notion at once. Does such a humble and wretched creature as myself, lost these past hours hopelessly, look as though she would harm, save but in feeble self-defense?"

Ian Farthing leaned over, allowing the torch to flicker over the creature. "Well, you are certainly big enough! Though I admit that if you wanted to attack, you would have done so by now."

"Indeed, good sir," said the creature calling herself Alison, "How reasonable you are. I knew I recognized a compassionate soul when I laid eyes upon your visage!"

"Well, I don't know what to say, except . . . wait a moment. You understand what I'm saying. No one understands me this well, except for my friend Hillary, and she's known me a long time!"

"Let's just say," said the monstrous woman, rising up from her crouching position, "that I have certain talents, one of 'em being a sort of ability to understand all languages—even Cleft Palate."

Not groveling now, with a shred of dignity and humanity to clothe herself in, Ian could see that she was indeed a woman—though as ugly as seven sins. She was tall and wide, and her breasts were quivery mountains in a bumpy range that included her head, hips, and backside bulging from the formless bundle of rags that served as a dress.

Then Ian identified her. She was some kind of hag, without a doubt. The stories that Ian had heard in Mullshire were rich with mentions of these strange and fickle branches of ensorceled humanity. Hags were variously shaped and sized, but they were seldom good things. But then, perhaps this was because of human prejudice—from hard experience, Ian Farthing knew that beauty was too often equated with wholesomeness, deformity with evil.

He would give this wretched hag the chance she requested.

"My name is Ian Farthing," he said. "I, along with my companions, are on a quest for a princess lost to this insane time."

The hag's eyes grew wide and burned within her moon face like ignited craters. "Princess! I don't want to hear about no princess! I've 'ad a stomach full of princesses. I've had enough of princesses to last me a godling's lifetime! Why, if it weren't for a princess, I might still be ensconced in comfort with my handsome dragoon, living in splendor and beauty!"

She sniffled, drew out a clotted handkerchief, and honked her nose.

Ian perked up. Could it be possible?

"I'm sorry, Alison . . . what did you say your last name was?"

"Gross, sir. Alison Gross."

"Yes . . . Mistress Gross. You said something about a princess. By any chance was this princess quite beautiful, with long blond hair and dressed in a gown?''

The hag eyed Ian thoughtfully. "Yes, and she called herself Alandra and said she was a virgin, though upon my life, she weren't, though my dear Princerik believed her.''

"Princerik?''

"Aye, my dear love, King of Crag's Keep. And I was its queen—until that bratty bitch showed up with her mangy cat. Caught the eye of my Princerik, she did, and it collected her straightaway and ensconced her in the Keep, and she hated me at first sight, and had me kicked from my beloved halls with all my friends and precious things. Kicked out to wander, wretched, through these tangled lands!''

The hag wrung her swarthy long-nailed hands.

Ian was stunned, aghast with hope.

"That's her!'' he was finally able to say, fidgeting with excitement. "That's the princess we're after!''

The hag shook with contained rage. "A pox on her pale skin!'' Her face mottled undelicate colors; then she somehow gagged herself, causing her shriek to die into a gentler tone. "You understand, kind savior, that she is the cause for my woes, and I do not have many gentle thoughts for the lady, valued as she may be to you.''

Ian's mind was racing; he barely heard her. "Tell me more about this Keep,'' he demanded eagerly.

The hag relaxed. "You will give me food and let me sit by your fire?''

"Of course! But you must tell us all that we need to know!'' Ian cried, almost shaking with delight. What a joyful happenstance! A gift from

God Himself, surely, showing His favor on their quest!

"Aow! Excellent," said the creature. "And you will be a dear and carry my bag, won't you? I'm quite exhausted after my trek!" She parted her hair and gave him a wink and a flirty air-kiss, then belched. "Oh my, excusez-moi!" Her giggles were on the obscene side.

Ian collected the firewood, accepted the hag bag, and staggered back to the knight's camp, saying, "You'd better let me go in first, Alison. I think I'll have to make a few explanations about you!"

All six knights stood, sat, or knelt on one side of the campfire, bristling with drawn weapons as they warily eyed the creature across from them, who was slavering and drooling with hunger.

"Oh, thank you, thank you so much!" cooed the hag as she chomped on one final morsel of food. "You gentlemen have been so kind to a destitute lady!" Apple juice spilled down the side of her chin, matted with cake crumbs clinging to her whiskers. She drew back a length of hair and pouted in what she thought was a seductive fashion, thrusting her immense droopy breasts out at them. "But whatever are you bold fellows doing yonder? Why don't you come over and keep a poor little ole girl company? I'd just love to thank you boys"—her voice grew breathy, husky—"any way I can!"

The knights scooted back a bit, raising their weapons defensively.

Alison Gross leaned over toward Ian and Hillary. "Tell me, are these boys queer?"

"Pardon?" Hillary said innocently.

"Oh, no," said Ian, not wanting to offend the hag and lose the information and guidance they needed. "They're just tired . . . and quite suspicious of strangers. I mean, when you're traveling through a strange and weird land and you come upon a beautiful woman . . . you have to be careful not to be seduced!"

Mollified, the hag straightened, primping away any hurt feelings. "Why yes, of course, I do see what you mean! Any closer and my beautiful scent might drive them into a sexual frenzy!"

Hillary caught on.

"Oh, my yes! I am keeping my eye on Ian every moment he's close to you!"

The hag sniggered and picked her nose.

It had taken some work to convince the company of knights that this lumpy, ugly mockery of human femininity should leave the forest without the benefit of arrows and daggers pincushioning her. But the notion of a speedy end to this quest plus expert aid in entering the halls of Alandra's imprisonment finally convinced at least Sir Godfrey of the wisdom of allowing Alison Gross entrance into their company.

"So then . . . madam," Sir Godfrey said, pronouncing the last word with deserved reluctance. "We have allowed you sanctuary from the cold and danger, as is your wish. You have supped and seem comfortable. Perhaps you would care to recount to us how you find yourself wandering in this magical wilderness and how you know the Princess Alandra. Master Ian Farthing tells us that you can tell us exactly where the princess is, and might just possibly guide us there and upon arrival assist us in liberating the lady!"

"You better believe it, buster!" said Alison

Gross, smacking her lips happily. "That tramp has got to go so my cherished Princerik will put me back in my rightful place near its heart."

"Princerik is apparently the master of the Keep I told you about," Ian explained. Hillary hastily translated as the lad expounded. "It's some form of dragon, living in a series of caverns atop a mountain, perched in a way that is difficult to reach without wings."

"And with these wings, this Princerik presumably carried Mistress Gross here and tossed her away," said Sir Godfrey.

"I wonder why," said Sir Oscar Cornwall drolly, staring, still amazed at the hag's loathsomeness.

"Because Princerik was ensorceled by the witch—what else?" cried Alison Gross. "Why else would my beloved dragoon act in such a fashion? How can you possibly even ask that question?"

"So then," said Sir Mortimer. "Perhaps you'd like to relate your story!" His blade was lowered, and his eyebrows were lifted with interest.

"I have a better idea!" the hag said exuberantly, bumbling to her feet, her rags shaking, breasts and belly bulging intimidatingly, causing Ian to scoot back to avoid being flattened. "I shall show you."

"Show us?" Hillary said. "What do you mean?"

"Oh, of course!" she said, a condescending smile growing on her thick, warty lips. "You are Outlanders. You have no magic about you by nature. Though sakes alive, I sense something strongly magical hereabouts. Well, no matter, this is all in the way of explanation." As she spoke, she slipped her clawed hand inside her ragged dress and commenced fiddling with buttons. Eventually, a protuberant greenish belly was exposed to the firelight, featuring a cavernous belly button. "My particular magic is not large and nothing to be frightened of certainly, you wonderful strapping lads! But as they say, pictures are worth a thousand words."

Without further ado, she plunged her right hand into her navel. A sucking sound later, her arm was all the way up to the elbow in flesh. The hag's face contorted as she groped about inside her guts. "Damn! Where has that thing gotten to?" Her features brightened. "Ah! There you are, you rascal."

She began to pull something out.

The questers could only stare in astonishment.

Slowly, Alison Gross tugged something from her abdomen into the open air. It shone wet and glistening in the firelight, attached by a length of red-and-purple flesh, veins pulsing. Ian could see that it was jewel-bright, like a knot of thick glass rope, with clouds of milky white swirling within.

"In God's name," gasped Sir Ronald Komquatte. "What is that?"

Alison Gross beamed proudly as she looked down at the item like a proud mother gazing at a baby still attached to its umbilical. "Why, honey, it's my Crystal Bowel, of course. Not real powerful, but I like it. Stores images of the past, and an occasional glimmer of the future! Well, come on over and take a look, fellows! It's not going to bite!"

Fascinated, the knights got up and moved closer, craning their necks for the best view from the most distant possible position. Ian and Hillary stared at the glimmery, shimmery thing, and Ian could see that, yes, it looked indeed like a coil of large intestine, only composed entirely of crystal.

"Let me see, now I just have to concentrate upon my memories and something should happen," Alison Gross said, closing her eyes.

As soon as the lids were down, the clouds began to collect into a solid congealed cream color.

A picture began to focus.

It showed Alison the hag leaning provocatively against the side of a beast half warped man, half dragon, twice her size. In the background were a number of stalagtites and stalagmites; clearly the pair were in a cavern of some sort.

"This is me and Princey," said Alison Gross. "Isn't it wonderful?" Stylized hearts began to float through the scene, and the image assumed a pink tint.

"Terribly big," muttered Sir Mortimer through his mustache.

"And I was very happy in its family!" Alison Gross continued. "I kept house, I helped cook, we played games . . . let me show you some more of the family!"

Ian watched as pictures paraded across the rounded face of the Crystal Bowel. What a motley collection of creatures, he thought. A true bestiary if he'd ever seen one! The hag spoke their names as their images flashed, and Ian marveled that such a variety of things could live in harmony. And such a collection of nasty-looking brutes at that!

"All was fine," continued the hag, "until she showed up."

And upon the face of the Crystal Bowel appeared the face that Ian Farthing knew he would never forget. Long blond hair dived in swirls down a face of rare perfection, centered by two ravishing blue eyes.

Ian could only sigh. "That's her," he said. "That's Alandra, all right!"

The knights jostled closer, eager for a look at the object of their quest. They suddenly stilled, stunned for a moment by the lady's beauty.

Ian remembered the first time he had seen her—as she had been galloping away from the Norx—and again that stunned, dizzy song sang in his head: love.

Godfrey stepped closer, eyes wide, reaching out as though to touch the image. "Mine!" he murmured, eyes a similar smoky glaze to the Crystal Bowel. "She's mine!"

"What in God's name do you think you're doing?" Alison Gross shrieked, tucking the device closer to home. "Don't touch the merchandise!"

Godfrey, startled, looked up at the hag's face, less than a foot away. The dull-eyed look cleared and an expression of horror took its place. Quickly, he jumped back, quite apparently more than a little confused.

"Yes, I realize how beautiful I am," said Alison Gross, "and I hate to turn away such a handsome specimen as yourself, but please, show a little discretion, Sir Knight!"

Hillary, noting the lost look hanging upon Ian like a spell, changed the subject. "Mistress Gross— you spoke of peering into the future using your magical, uhm, device. Do you think we might get a glimpse of what we can expect?"

"Sorry, dearie," said the hag. "But I'm feeling a

little constipated tonight. What with all my woe, don't you know." Lovingly, she roped her intestines back into place, then tucked her charm back inside her bulging abdomen and rebuttoned her navel. "Perhaps if we find some prunes later on!" She showed rotting teeth in a smile. "You've heard of reading tea leaves, haven't you, honey? Sometimes I can read—"

"I think we'd prefer the straighter stuff," interrupted Hillary.

The knights seemed to recover. Aghast at their nearness to this foul female, they stumbled over each other in their haste to get away. Only Sir Godfrey managed to contain his disgust and retain his place. "Please excuse my men, Mistress Gross. But they have taken vows of chastity," he said slyly, regaining his aplomb after his glimpse at Alandra, "and no doubt are sore tempted by a lady so charming as yourself."

Alison Gross preened, hawked up a gob of phlegm, and spat self-confidently. "Ah, I knew it must be something like that. I know how hard it is to resist such simmering sexuality as is mine, such seductive beauty! Truly, I do not know what spell that bitch-witch Alandra has placed on my dear Princerik to make it prefer her to me. Ah, if only I were to have the chance to deal with her!"

"Yes, well, we rather thought we'd give you that opportunity, Mistress Alison," Sir Godfrey continued in his silk-smooth voice. "You say that your friend Princerik threw you out of its Keep. Do you think you might find that Keep again?"

"Oh yes, without a redoubt!" Her giggle sounded like the last bit of sewage draining down a pipe.

"Then doubtless you would be willing to help

guide us there and help us remove your rival so that this spell can be broken and you may once more take your rightful place!"

"Oh serendipity!" the hag cried. "Oh fraptious day!" Drooling with happiness, she reached forward and grabbed Sir Godfrey and mashed his face between her mountainous breasts. "I have prayed for a valiant knight to succor me in my hour of need."

After a moment of muffled struggle, Sir Godfrey managed to pull himself loose. "No succoring involved, please, or anything to do with sucking, madam. Please remember that I too have taken vows of abstinence!" Struggling for breath, he stepped away from the hag's reach. "If we are to coexist in this journey, you must desist in your seductive ways."

Ian noted that the knight seemed to be having difficulty in his efforts not to gag.

"Forgive me, sir knight," said Alison Gross. "I was just so excited at the thought of being reinstated. Be warned, though, that the path is not an easy one, and to obtain the Keep of Princerik, much effort must be expended!"

"We have our mission and intend to keep our faith! Is this not true, Ian?" Sir Godfrey stepped forward and slammed a palm against Ian's back, nearly sending him sprawling to the ground.

"Er . . . yes, Godfrey. We must carry on the quest for the sake of Alandra and Mullshire . . . and from the sounds of it, the entire land," Ian stated, and Hillary translated.

"Yes, and the Princess Alandra is my intended. Were it not for some cosmic gaffe, even now she might be in my arms." He turned his head away, and for a moment Ian saw some true tender emotion cross the knight's face. Flickerings of sympathy and jealousy intertwined stirred in him, for he knew what emotions Godfrey must be enduring after catching a glimpse of such beauty; yet he fain would have the princess for himself.

Stupid lumpneck, he told himself. Why would a princess have anything to do with you? Especially after what happened at Jat's Pass.

"Enough excitement," said Sir Godfrey. "We must have some rest. I'm sure you are quite tired after what you have endured, Mistress Gross. But we must ask that you occupy a place downwind . . . ah, I mean away from most of us so that my knights will not be tempted to stray from their vows."

"Just give me a place to rest these weary bones, and I shall be a happy damosel indeed." She frumped and bumped her way to a place by the fire, then keeled over and wobbled on the ground. "Ah, sweet bliss, to know I shall return to my lovely Princerik."

Almost immediately a snore like thunder in a mudpile began.

"Ah well, as the saying goes, the mixed blessing is a blessing nonetheless," said Godfrey. "Ian, truly, I am proud of you. Light at the end of the tunnel perhaps, eh?"

"We are quite fortunate," returned Ian.

"I confess, I am too excited by these events to sleep yet, so I shall take the first watch," said Sir Godfrey. "Now you two take your sleep! We must get our rest, no?"

"We'll do our best, Godfrey," said Hillary. She

tugged Ian to their sleeping bags. "Come, Ian. You've had your day's worth of excitement, I think."

Ian Farthing agreed quite readily and followed his dear friend to bed.

chapter four

Oespite his fatigue, Ian Farthing could not sleep.

He lay in his bedsack, beneath the stars and the dice-shaped moons and the curling lines of the world slashing across the sky, aching and itching, wishing he were somewhere else entirely. This poor body simply wasn't built to withstand adventure, he thought. Not these crooked legs and arms, this bent back, these ugly features. God had surely intended him solely for cobbler work, and now he was defying God and suffering for it.

Moaning, he turned over, trying to find a comfortable position bereft of stones or twigs, trying to snuggle down into a dreamland far less fantastic than the one that his party traipsed through now.

"Ian!" called a voice. "Ian, if you make another sound or sob or moan again, so help me, I'll put you to sleep by braining you with one of these rocks."

Ian recognized the voice. Hillary could be so subtle sometimes.

"Do it. Maybe it will help me sleep," he replied miserably.

"Oh, Ian," Hillary said, scooting herself closer to him. He could barely make out her form by the moonlight, but he could sense her presence, feel her warm breath against his face, detect her unmistakable girlish smell. "What am I going to do with you? We're on the most exciting of missions, you're getting the chance you've always wanted to prove your worth, and you're acting as though you're on the road to Hell itself!"

"Feels like Hell, it does, Hiller," Ian snuffled miserably, letting the day's sights and frights finally sink in. "I'm just not cut out to be a hero or to go questing or anything remotely like this bloody nonsense."

"Well, you've no choice about it, do you? So go to sleep and we'll talk in the morning." She turned away from him huffily, assuming a sleeping position, not letting him have the final say.

Not that he had anything to say that she hadn't already heard today. In truth, even Ian was tired of all his groanings and complaints, his twitchiness, his nervousness. It was as though he couldn't help it, any more than he could help being where he was now, a reluctant hero if ever there was one.

Reluctant zero would be a better term, he thought morosely. Where is that friendly voice in my head that saved me from the Norx, that drove me forward against that hand halting the knights' progress into the Dark Land? In my moments of true need, it abandons me.

He dwelt on that awhile, and he let himself listen for that Voice, closing his eyes in the hope perhaps of catching a glimpse of its spectral presence . . . but found only a deeper darkness behind his lids than existed in the starry night.

Damn. Even Hillary, faithful friend and boon
companion, was sick of him. And he couldn't
blame her, what with the kind of whining he put
up as a cushion against himself and reality. And
he really couldn't blame her. He just had to stop
it, he just had to take her advice and the advice of
the Voice and believe in himself, for God's sake.
She was right, dammit! He should realize that
there was more to him than just a gangly collection of faults strung together by a whine. All this
business about being homesick for the "comfort"
of his cobbling trade was nonsense as well. It was
cramped and wretched and tiring work for which
he got precious little money and even less appre-
ciation. But it was what he knew, and so he
accepted it blindly and by sheer habit wanted it
back. He was being a real idiot. What other
Mullshire lad ever got the chance to pull himself
from the dregs, to strike out for some exciting if
uncomfortable destiny?

Besides, from all accounts, he wasn't really who
he thought he was, anyway.

He had to find out the truth, no matter what it
was, no matter what the cost.

Consoling himself that he was at least partially
confronting the truth, Ian allowed his tense muscles to relax somewhat, and he felt his insides
unwind, and he felt his mind drifting into some-
place soft and nice and familiar and—

"Ian?"

Instantly, Ian Farthing was awake. "Who . . .
what . . . ?" he said, completely tense again. He
was sick with alertness.

"Ian. She is very beautiful."

Ian blinked, recognizing Hillary's voice. He relaxed somewhat. "Hiller, don't be daft. Of course

she's beautiful. She's a princess. Now let me get some sleep. I was just in the middle of a doze!"

"Ian, you love her, don't you?" Hillary's voice was tense and accusatory. "You want her for yourself!"

Ian was too close to slumber to be dishonest. "Guess I wouldn't mind," he pronounced dreamily.

A small fist suddenly connected with his arm, wielding considerable force. "You rotten person you!"

Ian grunted. "Hiller! Cut it out!"

"She's no good, I can tell it, Ian. No good for you, mark my words!"

"Hiller, I didn't want to go after her, remember? I chickened out. Besides, this quest is as much to save Mullshire as to save Alandra. And anyway, Sir Godfrey has a rightful claim to her, magically and, from the looks of it, emotionally. What's got into you?"

"I don't know, Ian," she said, her huffiness diminishing. "I just got . . . I don't know, inflamed there for a moment. I guess . . . I guess you mean a lot to me, and I saw how beautiful Alandra was in that Crystal Bowel, and I got jealous. I suppose I was just concerned for you."

"You're my friend, Hiller. I'm not going to forget about you. Besides, can you see Princess Alandra falling for a prize like me?"

"If it's looks you're speaking of, you have changed since we entered the Dark Circle, Ian. You're straighter, and your features have . . . evened. What if you get even better? What if you become handsome and dashing? You'll just ditch me, won't you?"

"Ditch you? How?"

"I don't know, Ian. I just don't know. Ian, how about me? Do you love me?"

"Love you? I don't know—I haven't thought about it much. I guess so, Hiller. We've known each other too long—I've never been apart from you. How am I—"

"Just shut up, Ian," she said, turning over. "Go back to sleep and forget the whole thing."

Ian shrugged and obeyed, this time finding her order not too hard to obey at all.

Distantly, he heard a rustling, but he ignored it.

chapter five

... the barbarian wielded his broadsword as
though the shaft of nicked iron were one with the
mighty thews of his arms. His eyes flashed as the
wizard crafted another desperate fireball from
the sulfurous air, then hurled it toward the hero
from the North.

The fire hurled through the sulfurous air like a
screaming demon. "Grub!" cried Canine the Barbarian, invoking his God of the Frosty Reaches.
Canine held up his mighty sword, deflecting fire,
which hissed into the misty swamp.

"Now, Blackheart," he growled. "Taste good
honest metal!" His rocky muscles propelled him
toward the robed miscreant, and his broadsword
descended upon the weakened field of sorcery.
Sparks crackled and twirled as the sword sliced
through the bluish-red aura and hacked into the
sorcerer's shoulder.

Blackheart screamed. Blood spurted as the sorcerer tried to wrench the sword from his body
with his bare hands—

"Damn it!" the Dark Lord cried, hurling the yellowed paperback across the room. It hit the wall

and tumbled back into the crate of books from which it had come. "Balthazar's balls, why do these wretches always win?" The mattress squeaked as the Dark Lord rose to get himself another beer.

Roth Kogar knew bloody well that these books, with their bizarrely muscled heroes and their garish monsters, mostly believable and realistic enough, copped out in the end, dissolving into ludicrous fantasy—but still, ever since he had discovered the library cache, they were among his favorite reading material. Especially now that he had so much time to kill in his little Sleeping Spell module, his prison, his cell within his own manse, sequestered there by Morgsteen all this time.

As the Dark Lord walked across the tattered Pakistani carpet, he scratched his protruding belly through a stained sleeveless undershirt and snarled to himself. Once! he thought. Just once I'd like to see one of those barbarians get what they'd really get if they went up against the likes of me!

Just the same, he knew he'd finish the book and maybe shed a few tears for Blackheart—the stories weren't so bad if you considered them tragedies like Hamlet or Oedipus Rex. Hell, yes— stories of villains with faults that ultimately tripped them up. Too, they were almost like dry runs for the Dark Lord. By the time a jerk like Canine the Barbarian thudded and blundered across Roth Kogar's path, you could bet that the Dark Lord wouldn't waste any time taking away that bloody broadsword!

The Dark Lord grunted as he opened his refrigerator, kept cold by a charm, and pulled out a long-necked bottle of Budweiser. Like the books, he'd found the beer out in the wastelands of the Dark Circle, detritus from a world he found most fascinating. His minions had located cases upon cases of the brew, and Kogar soon formed an addiction to it. He was most grateful that he'd stocked it in this emergency room, his falling-out shelter so to speak.

He used his teeth to open the bottle and took a thirsty gulp of the fizzy stuff, eyes glancing about at the heaps of food and beer and books and junk he'd collected in this chamber. Could be worse, he mused. It'll take me years just to sort through all this mess. Indeed, there were boxes that hadn't even been opened yet, all found in clumps within the Dark Circle, refugees from wherever.

There were paintings and magazines, tea services and totems. There were silverware and kiddie toys, fireworks and sports equipment. He'd never had time to sort through all this mess before when he'd been busy trying to conquer the whole of the Dark Circle with the other Dark Lord, Morgsteen. Now, alas, he had plenty of time, thanks to Snirk Morgsteen.

Kogar took a furious gulp of his brew at the very thought of his former ally. Foam spilled into his black beard, and his solid black pupils seemed to turn molten. Betrayed! The very word caused his simmering inner fires to flare up again. Betrayed by that simpering worm! The ignominy, the shame!

It had taken years for the two to finally come to terms, to put away their differences and ally against the Bright Lords, and finally to defeat them by force and trickery. And then that slimy toad Morgsteen had triggered the network of spells

hidden in Kogar's castle, nearly destroying him.
If he hadn't prepared this room for just such a
possibility, he would have had no place to retreat
to, no sanctuary. Morgsteen's magicians had woven
their sleeping spell about this cocoon, true . . .
but they could not get in or otherwise affect him
because of the sorcerous power of a certain jewel
Kogar kept within the cell. Thus it was a stale-
mate—at least, until Kogar had managed to get
his radio equipment cobbled together, activate
his robot doppleganger, interpret the cosmic read-
ings sufficiently to fly in his ornithopter with his
Marines and find the woman called Alandra, and
thus obtain the power he needed not only to get
out of this mess, but to regain his kingdom.

Roth Kogar sighed. He slumped into a chair,
leaned over, and picked out his paperback again.
He took another sip of beer and put it on a clut-
tered coffee table.

His one hope lay with that ragtag bunch of
knights and that strange young man. They thought
he was held in a sleeping spell, which was just as
well . . . and not far bloody wrong.

As though on cue, the red light on his radio
equipment blipped and speakers issued a staticky
grumble. Kogar flicked his eyes up and saw that
he was being summoned. It would be late now in
the camp of the questing party, so he knew who it
had to be. . . .

Kogar went and sat by his equipment, a mish-
mash of radio coils, knobs, dials, and tubing all
held together by strange magical conglomerations
like troll teeth and medusa stone. The stuff seemed
to ooze over the countertop, like a melting or-
ganic radio set. Kogar took another pull from his

beer, sat down before his sole contact with the outside world, and plugged himself in.

This operation consisted of pulling out ropes of intestinelike tubing and affixing them to his ears, his mouth, and, after taking a moment to secure the proper tuning, his eyes, transforming all to darkness and silence. Then slowly his consciousness dissolved through to the sound of a distant fire crackling, the whicker of horses, the creak of wind through tree branches, and the sight of a man's face looking down at him.

"Greetings again, Dark Lord," said the man. "I am sorry to disturb your sleep, but a matter has arisen that merits your attention."

"By Zeus's mucus," said Roth Kogar, "it had better be good. This takes a great deal out of me, you know!"

"Yes, of course, and I would have waited until the morrow, but there are matters that I should like to deal with that should not fall on others' ears."

Kogar grinned to himself. "You mean our little arrangement, sir knight?"

"Quite. I'm on guard duty, and the others are asleep, so we can speak candidly."

"First, what has happened?"

"We know where Alandra is, and we are being led there by a hag. I shall not bore you with the whole story, but suffice it to say that with the combination of your aid and hers, our likelihood of a quick and successful completion of this quest increases amazingly."

"Excellent!"

"And when we rescue the princess, we shall come to your aid—but, of course, that is part of the deal."

"Yes."

"And I shall, as you promised, have a whole kingdom to rule."

"That is indeed our personal deal, once I make use of the Key. But what more do you need to know, sir knight, that is not already agreed to?"

"I merely wish to make sure of one thing, Lord Kogar. I had before been happy with the assumption . . . but I should like it made clear."

"And what is that? Speak up, and we shall see."

"I wish . . ." The knight cleared his voice. "The hag magically conjured a vision of the Princess Alandra this eve. I fear the very sight of her has made a slave of my heart. I wish to have her as my own, Roth Kogar. I wish to make her my bride once she is rescued and the balances of power are tilted in our favor. I cannot sleep until you give me that assurance."

Roth Kogar laughed. "Such a silly thing! But of course, sir knight. There is no difficulty whatsoever. I shall make certain that she is yours, in return for your sworn loyalty to me and your promise that you shall carry out all the deeds that I have asked of you. There must be none left to challenge me after I successfully control the Key, you understand?"

The knight chuckled. "I understand."

"The others are needed to aid us in our mission, but they shall be hindrances or even threats to us if allowed to go their ways after the end of the quest."

"They shall meet their ends, I promise, Lord Kogar. That request will not be difficult to carry out."

"See that it is carried out. I anticipate no diffi-

culty at all. Except for that little fellow. There is
threat to us all there, Sir Knight. I feel it, yea,
even from here, through the head you clutch in
your hands."

"His end will give me especial pleasure, Lord
Kogar. But as you say, he will be useful—"

"Until I say he is of no use! We must be careful
lest he gains too much knowledge, too much
power."

"Knowledge, you say. Could you pray impart
some more of that to me? I am still too much in
the dark concerning the forces that swirl about
this world."

"In time, sir knight. In time. But I grow weary,
and I have other matters to turn my concentration
to. Farewell. If the head works properly tomorrow, I shall address you all. I should like particularly to speak to this magical hag you have told
me of."

"Your will is my command, oh lord," said the
knight.

"The others do not suspect your complicity
with me, then?"

"They do not, oh lord, nor will they. And if I
should detect any such suspicion, I shall see that
that individual meets with a fatal accident."

"Excellent. I have chosen wisely. Rest well, sir
knight . . . and be assured that treasures and glories beyond your imagination will be yours with
our success!"

"I shall only be happy if I can share them with
Alandra," were the knight's final words before
Kogar disconnected.

The romantic fool, the Dark Lord thought. The
silly goon.

He replaced the operational devices of his part-magical, part-technological equipment and shuddered. Being in full control of his robot self had been liberating—but being inside just a head gave the Dark Lord the creepy-crawlies!

Roth Kogar regarded his cell with satisfaction. "I shall be sure that I use this place as a torture dungeon for you, Snirk Morgsteen. And I shall revel in all your agonies."

The Dark Lord went for another beer, parked himself in a chair, picked up his paperback book, and continued to read.

chapter six

In the morning, they ventured onward.

Their pace was slowed, since Alison Gross, the hag, had no horse and none of the knights, not even Ian Farthing, nor Hillary Muffin was willing to allow the foul and weighty thing either to share a saddle or to borrow a mount. However, with the assurance that their goal was within reach, and treasuring the knowledge of that goal's whereabouts, they attacked their task of journeying with added optimism.

This was fortunate, for, in general, the landscape became increasingly dangerous and increasingly strange.

Ian immediately noted that the land grew gradually less dark and dreary as they traveled deeper toward what had, before the Change, been its center. Mountains seemed to be gentling down to hills and valleys; the land was composed more of forest and meadows than bleak and ravaged terrain. Yet these new features by no means normalized the look of things, for they were overcast by an air of difference. They were colored differently, their smells had an odd effervescence of expectation—an

imminence of something happening, something
wonderful and bizarre, any moment now!

Their procession was orderly and generally quiet
in between the fantastic incidents that sprang up
around them like weeds in the garden. Fortunately, none of these incidents called for their attention, being sideshow affairs of images flickering
from other worlds, satyrs being chased by nymphs,
fantasy worlds gone totally mad. Ian watched all
these progressions of images like the mystery and
miracle plays he enjoyed so much back home.
They seemed full of content and hurly-burly, these
panoplies part mirage and part live action. Yet,
truly, he didn't know what the hell they meant—if
they meant anything at all.

"Don't pay no attention," Alison Gross suggested. "I've seen this sort of thing before. The air
is just settling down from the shakeup. There's
nothing to fear—you're just peering into different
worlds, or seein' confused stuff accustom itself to
the new way things look here, which ain't easy,
let me tell you!"

Ian certainly had to agree with that thought.
Although the ground seemed normal enough as
their horses clopped along the frazzled roads, the
horizons before or behind them looped up and
over, roller-coaster-style. Curiously enough, although the planetary configuration was now different, the sun still rose in the morning and set in
the evening, just where it used to . . . only in that
former horizon now lay only sky and clouds. The
same was true for the dice-moons, eternally rolling in the heavens, playing their silent celestial
game.

"That's the problem with this infernal place,"
said Alison Gross at one point. "It's totally arbi-

trary. Everything and everybody is from some-place else! You've got bits and pieces from different worlds—it's a damned patchwork world is what it is! That's why it's so hard to keep a family together, which is why I cherished my dear Princerik!''

She sighed, but brightened when reminded that she would be returned forthwith to her home, and the object of her hatred would, with her help, be removed.

By day, Alison Gross was, if anything, uglier. The other knights kept their distance, trudging along cold-eyed, weapons ready for the odd chimera or lion, tiger or bear they expected to attack them at any time, but Ian and Hillary, no strangers to hideous things, kept close, eager to learn what the hag knew of this strange and magical clime.

"Not as much as I'd like to, I'll tell you that," she responded to a direct question on the second day, chomping on a batch of strange weed she'd discovered growing by the side of the road. "Here ye go, Ian," she said, dragging a healthy dollop from her mouth and offering the lad the stuff, dripping with spittle. "Dope wort. Good for what ails ya!" She winked a sty-covered eye at Hillary. "I know about all the plants that grow here in the Dark Circle, and this here's my favorite. You wouldn't have a pipe on ya, would ya?"

Ian waved away the offering. "You seem to know quite a bit about this place, actually, Mistress Gross, so even if you feel yourself ignorant, we still would benefit from your shreds of knowl-edge."

Alison Gross shrugged and tossed the chomp of weed back into her mouth. "Mebbe you'd like some Merrie January better." She spat out a squirt of juice. "Well now, what kin ah tell ya that you might not know?"

"Who exactly is this Alandra, and whyever is she so important?" Hillary piped up insistently.

"Why, hell if I know, my dear," Alison Gross said, coughing. "Just a little hussy, far as I kin tell. Looks like she could service Dooper's Troopers in an easy evenin'. But I hear things, and I feel things, and definitely there's something magical about that bitch, otherwise she wouldn't have been able to snitch my Princerik away!"

"No, I think that Hillary wants some background on this princess, and on Roth Kogar, and on just what's going on, Mistress Gross."

"Oh, that awful head!" the hag said, shuddering. The two had come face to face the morning after their encounter, and though Kogar had seemed glad of the additional help in guiding the party, Alison Gross had taken a decided dislike to the thing. "Ain't nothin' right 'bout a head that ain't got no body to hang to, mark my words. But I heard of Kogar, oh yes, I heard of Snirk Morgsteen as well. They're the Dark Lords, and they've been fightin' for control of this land for years, and lately they've been makin' it, too. But you're right—there is something mighty fishy going on." Her tangled mop of hair fluttered as she shivered with her entire massive body—a profound sight indeed.

"You must understand, Mistress Gross," said Ian, "that Hillary and I come from a very sheltered existence outside the circle. We're just normal folk, living normal lives—and all of this talk of wizards and magic used to just belong in the stories we heard."

Alison Gross nodded her head understandingly.

"Aye, and I've been protected meself these past years, sheltered by Princerik's keep. But I've heard stories, too—stories about wizards much more powerful than the common lot runnin' 'bout here scratchin' and peckin' for power like hens in a barnyard. Stories about wizards who game like the gods with our lives and the powers hereabouts. Well, I know it sounds like stuff and nonsense, but there's got to be some reason the world's turned topsy-turvy like this."

"It does sound—bizarre," said Hillary, "but it ties in very neatly with what's happened, and besides, think about those moons!"

Ian shook his head forlornly. "I would just like to go home."

"And that's where I'm goin'," said Alison Gross gleefully. "With your kind help, of course. Say," she said, reaching into her rag-heap dress for her Crystal Bowel. "Would you like to have another look at the place? Maybe we'll get a look-see at the future, too. Had a right good squat this mornin' that portends good things!"

Ian and Hillary hastily assured her that they only wished a verbal spillage of guts.

And so the journey continued onward through the chiaroscuro landscape, wild visions still riding the air like draperies of dreams, glimpses of strange creatures skulking through woods and behind rocks, but never attacking, as though they too were thoroughly confused with the changes in their magical lands and had, for a time, forgotten their monsterly duties.

Ian was, for the most part, dizzy or ill or just plain nervous; only Hillary was able to calm him. He had developed a case of the piles that was adding acute discomfort to his general misery; he gave up his horse from time to time to Alison Gross so that he could walk, a preferable state to riding in agony.

"Remember, Hillary," he said on the evening of the third day after meeting Alison Gross, "we used to hear all those wondrous stories about brave travelers and glorious quests? They never ever mentioned how uncomfortable it can be!"

His head was lying in her lap. She looked down at him and said, "They never said it was comfortable, Ian. Why does it have to be?"

"I·mean, all these stories," Ian said, excited that he was finding words to fit his jittery emotions. "They make it sound so wonderful ... even death is wonderful, and pain is there, but it's quick. Questing is a tedious, miserable business! I even heard the other knights complaining today."

"I suppose one can get used to it, Ian," returned Hillary.

"Are you used to it?" Ian demanded.

"I'm here with you, Ian. We're doing something very brave and worthwhile. Isn't that enough?" Firelight flickered over her face and red hair, and she looked somehow much more grown-up now than her years would imply. "Whoever promised you that anything would be comfortable in life? Seems to me, Ian, that we should be grateful."

"Grateful! Are you daft, Hiller? We're out in the middle of the bloody Dark Circle gone gaga. Mullshire, our home, is in tatters. Whyever should we be grateful?"

She smiled wryly. "Because we have a purpose. A mission, Ian. Something to work toward, something valuable and straightforward and ... well, good. Our lives mean something." She rubbed his head affectionately. "Besides, I get to be with you, silly—why shouldn't I be grateful? Granted, I'm not comfortable either. I miss my mother and my father and my home. I'm weary of traveling, and I certainly do not care for this Princess Alandra at all. But all in all, I think that I am not unhappy. And I think that you invest too much importance in your own complaining!"

"Well, I've got plenty to complain about," said Ian.

"If you ask my opinion, Ian Farthing, I'd say it was just a habit. You just like to hear the sound of your own groans. Now go to sleep, so at least I won't have to hear about how tired you are tomorrow!"

Ian grudgingly gave up his place in her lap and found his leaf-strewn bedroll.

Just as he was drifting off, Hillary said, "Oh, and Ian, don't get vain about this or anything, but you are changing."

"Hmmph? What are you talking about, Hiller?" Ian said moodily, annoyed that he'd been yanked so abruptly from the edge of slumber.

"Maybe it's the magic in the air, Ian—I'm not sure," said Hillary softly. "But your features are getting more regular. You're standing just a little straighter. Other little things. It's like . . . well, I guess it's as though you've been destined to make this quest, Ian. And the closer you get to where you're supposed to be, the more you prove your true worth, the more beautiful you become. You've always wanted to look like other people, Ian. So think about that. Maybe, after all this is over, you will."

"Oh, sure, and hell will freeze over, too!" Ian grumbled.

But his heart leaped at the notion. He, Ian Farthing, handsome? Was it true? In fact, the knights seemed to understand him better, now that he thought of it. Perhaps Hillary was right, though it seemed too good to be true.

Besides, it was a scary thought as well. Somehow, it was more frightening than anything he'd encountered so far on this quest.

Ian Farthing—standing straight, without a clubfoot, without a hunched back and ugly face and bumps and maybe even a little taller and—

Exciting and unimaginable and scary.

In fact, he could not harbor the thought for very long at all, it burned his thoughts so badly. Ian Farthing. Different. A hero. Important.

What nonsense. It just wouldn't happen. He was an idiot, a fool—God's stumblebum. It was his role in life, as his parents told him, and you had to learn to accept your role, learn how you fit in the mosaic of things, do your duty, your job, lest the Devil himself tempt you—

The Devil. He hadn't thought about the Devil too much lately, with everything that had been happening, but now the thought and image of the leering rebel from Heaven consumed his attention. For the first time it occurred to him that by allowing events to carry him along so, he was being sucked into temptation of some sort. Demons clearly abounded in the Dark Circle. He'd seen their terrible faces in the moiling vision mists along the trail, and he imagined them skittering just out of sight, peering into his thoughts and chuckling at this bent little morsel of God they would consume at the first possible chance, these henchmen of Satan himself.

Perhaps that was the answer to all this lunacy—

this was all a part of Satan's plans ... the End Times.

But it was confusing, because despite the deep religious belief that had been branded into his brain by his life in Mullshire, all that he had seen and heard and experienced just did not add up into any kind of sense that could align with a Catholic view of the universe.

Or perhaps his mind was just too small to rationalize properly. Somewhere behind all this confusion was, if not rhyme and reason, then at least some scintilla of sense! God's plan must somehow be served!

"Dear God," prayed Ian Farthing to soothe himself toward slumber. "Get me out of this mess, and back into my comfortable shoe shop, and I'll never miss mass again!"

The only reply he seemed to hear was a faint whisper that seemed to be in his own voice: "Shut up and go to sleep, mush-head!"

chapter seven

though frights and dangers seemed to abound upon the path that Alison Gross and Roth Kogar guided them along, the party of questing knights did not actually encounter their first adventure fraught with any kind of fighting until the fourth morning.

However, the adventure proved to be absolutely beastly.

The skies seemed to have actually calmed down somewhat, the weird tapestries of sights and sounds abated, the cacophony of confused creatures lessened as all discovered that life, albeit strangely re-enchanted, went on.

The daylight had been accompanied by birdsong. The air seemed somehow sweeter, less murky with magic. Spirits among the knights seemed noticeably improved as they breakfasted and joked, then mounted their rested steeds and set out for their destinies.

Hillary actually felt spritely enough to sing a little ditty; Alison Gross droned along with her, adding her own verses. Even Kogar, when called up, seemed in good spirits, his voice vaguely slurred as though cheerily intoxicated, his pronouncements punctuated by the odd slurp and belch, which he assured everyone were a form of static in the magical radio waves.

Only Ian felt trepidation. But then, Ian Farthing always felt trepidation, and thus his voicings of gloom were laughed at by the knights, who were coming to understand him.

"Thank God we couldn't understand you so well before," said Sir Oscar Cornwall, his chain mail jingling as he turned around to Ian, smile wide on his thick face. "You've got nothing but pessimism sitting in that crooked skull of yours, Ian Farthing. Come on, cheer up and sing along with your little friend."

"Right," said Sir Mortimer Shieldson, scratching his mustache, a smile tugging at the corners of his usually morose mouth. "We've just been thinking, the boys and me, how that besides the glory and all that, there might be a good deal of treasure to be found at the end of this here quest. At the very least, this Princess Alandra is no doubt very rich and will reward us tremendously!"

" 'Tis true! 'Tis true!" said Sir Godfrey, eyes carrying an odd fire to them. "For how could such a gloriously beautiful woman be aught but generous? And I shall be principal beneficiary, as I am her intended and would surely have been her savior already except for Ian!" The knight glared at Ian, and with the kind of mood Ian was in, he felt like withering under the strong dark gaze.

"Stuff and nonsense!" trumpeted Hillary, giving the knight a fiery glance. "How do you know that something else might not have gone wrong, Godfrey Pinkham? Why, the Norx were right on her heels, from the sound of it! She was supposed to have galloped all the way to Mull without those creatures catching her? And how do you know you could have dealt with them, eh? They don't exactly sound puny, those Norx!"

"You know, girl," growled Sir Godfrey, "now that Master Farthing's speech problem has cleared up somewhat and we can make out what he's saying, we have little need for the likes of you. You'd best be aware of that and keep in your place!"

"Now Pinkham, have a care with your words," said Sir Oscar. "I think I speak for the rest of us when I say that we've all grown quite fond of Hillary. Fond and protective. So, leader you may be, but you'll not be threatening a friend—especially when she makes so good a point. No one else is challenging your right to claim the hand of Alandra Bellworthy, so you need not be so defensive. Little Hillary's mouth certainly is no threat to your vanity, and remember that you need us all for this quest to succeed."

"Hear hear!" cried two of the knights.

Sir Godfrey grumbled a bit, but he could offer no other words, so he fell into a pout and let the others continue their singing as the group wended on their merry way.

Hillary had just been asked to make up a song about Alison Gross when the troll stepped into their path, fully four yards tall, stocky and muscular as the most powerful of knights, only in much larger proportion, of course.

Instantly, swords rang out and arrows notched as the knights bristled into action, ready for an attack.

"Hallo there, brave travelers!" the troll called out in a surprisingly gentle and squeaky voice, with just a hint of a lisp. "I heard your songs and ventured out to wish you well!"

"Good God, he's huge!" said Sir Ronald Komquatte. "Golaith wouldn't hold a candle to him!" The knight raised his bow higher, but Sir Godfrey, alongside him, put a calming hand on the knight's raised arm.

"Weapons down, lads. Let's see what the giant has to say."

"In sooth, he's a troll and no giant. Why, take a look at that face!" said Alison Gross. "Ugly as Adam's sin. Giants are handsome louts."

"Aye," called the troll, "I certainly am a troll. Erasmus Trollkein, to be precise." The troll bowed in a most formal manner, then arose, his smile wrinkling further his already wrinkled and rough face, riddled with warts, tufted with patches of ugly brown and black hairs. "At your service. Dear people, forgive me for frightening you in this manner, for I realize that my stature is imposing and my countenance alarming. Truly, I mean no harm and I am certainly not armed." He extended bare, knobby hands to illustrate this truth. "To be perfectly honest, I am but a meek soul living here in the wild with my wife in a cottage yonder. We have little contact with the outside world, and so the events of the past few days have alarmed us greatly. I have intruded upon your journey to ask if you've any notion of just what might have happened in the cosmos to cause such a cataclysm."

The troll was dressed like a country gentleman, in tan corduroy trousers and waistcoat, and a jacket of matching material with brown patches on the elbows. He wore a floppy red bow tie beneath heavy jowls and carried a walking stick,

so that any fear derived from his wild thatch of
hair and ugly face was countered by his civilized
dress, his mild delivery, and his smile. A sun-
flower slipped into the button of a lapel further
underlined the impression of jolly benevolence.
Only the occasional flash of oversized canines (in
addition to the size and the ugliness, of course)
gave any sign of truly trollish tendencies.

As far as Ian Farthing was concerned, they
should give this guy a wide berth. But the others,
with the possible exception of Alison Gross,
seemed to be charmed by the feyness of the fellow.

"Honestly wish we could tell you, Mr. Troll,"
replied Sir Godfrey. "We're not entirely sure ourselves, are we, chaps? And it would take entirely
too long to inform you properly. But I will tell
you one thing, sir—we're on our way to put things
to right, and I myself to claim a fair maiden,
which is my right as the most valiant of knights."

"What ho! Oh my, and gracious me, a quest, a
quest!" cried Erasmus Trollkein, his thick stubby
fingers fluttering fumblingly at his starched shirt
collar like caterpillars aspiring toward butterfly-
hood. "Oh, how the missus and I admire quests!
Why, last century we entertained King Pellinore
in the midst of his search for the Questing Beasts!
And my great-great-grandfather served tea and
cakes to none other than Sir Galahad as he sought
the Holy Crock!"

"Grail, you mean?" offered Sir Godfrey.

"Oh, no, that was much later. This was a quest
you don't hear so much about. And what a crock
it proved to be!" His large reddened eyes almost
seemed to ignite as a thought occurred to him.
"But gentlepeople, you must be weary! My cottage is just around the bend, near the meadow.

The missus is even now baking a huge pie, and we've fresh scones and buckets of piping-hot tea with cream and butter and jam. Why, you must come and have a bit of a break in your travels! I'd ask you to stay the night, but we've simply no place to put you, but by all means come and have tea and tell us all about yourselves! A clearly first-class knight such as yourself deserves such treatment 'midst his travels and travails! And your friends, too! So please come!"

The sight of such a large and hideous troll almost beside himself with eagerness to please was something to behold. His bloodshot eyes bulged, his dewlaps quivered, his large pointy ears grew absolutely crimson as the ends of his smile almost seemed to touch them, showing off amazingly white teeth.

"What do you say, lads?" said Sir Godfrey, looking around at his companions. "A pleasant invitation from a pleasant fellow who seems to appreciate the nobility and importance of questers and questing."

"Aye!" said Sir Mortimer Shieldson. "I could do with a spot of tea, and the idea of a home-baked meal makes me stomach rumble!"

General murmurs of assent buzzed through the group.

"How do we know that you're a friendly troll?" demanded Alison Gross warily.

"Have I asked you for any payment to travel my road?" the troll countered, smile still firmly in place. "I am no toll troll, madam. You may be assured of that."

"There's certainly other kinds of trolls than toll trolls, mister," replied the hag.

"Yes, and you must see with your eyes that I

am no mole troll, for I do not live in the ground. And I do not play sports except for the odd bout of darts or croquet, so I am no goal troll. I am no midwife to horses, and therefore no foal troll."

"Then whatever are you?" screeched Alison.

"Why, I am a clever, funny, and happy troll, and therefore I am a droll troll," Erasmus Trollkein said, executing a fast soft-shoe and ending with his hat in his hand. "Now come on, chaps! We'd love the company."

"I'm not so sure about this, Godfrey," said Ian, leaning over in the leader's direction. "We're going to go back to that behemoth's hole? Why borrow trouble?"

For the first time, the troll frowned, and the effect was truly horrendous. "Nor am I a hole troll, sirrah! As I have said, the missus and I have a very nice cottage." The smile returned. "Oh, and did I mention, gentlemen, that I pride myself on my homemade daffodil wine? Very delicious, very potent stuff!"

"You know, Ian," said Sir Godfrey stiffly, "I suppose we should allow your little girlfriend to stay. I didn't understand a word you just said. Lead on, Mr. Witty Twit ... pardon me, Droll Troll. We should be happy to share tea and cakes with you and your missus ... but only for a time, mind you. We must be on our way for our glorious quest before too very long."

"Understood, understood!" the creature squeaked in near rapture, thick belly jouncing as he jumped in glee. "The missus and I will be speedy in our ministrations, I assure you." The troll blinked broadly. "You will not be sorry, I assure you."

"I don't know, Hiller. What do you think?" Ian

said as the troll skipped around and beckoned the knights to follow him off the roadway.

Hillary's eyes were glazed. "Tea!" she cooed. "Cakes!" Their supply of sweets had run out long before, and much of Hillary's talk, in between her little songs, had been of sweets and biscuits and all manner of good-tasting treats. "Why, goodness knows what goodies might await us here in this civilized section of the Dark Circle." She spoke with an enthusiasm that made it sound as though the discovery of new gustatory delights had been the principal reason she'd come along on the quest. "Ian, perhaps they will even let us take some along with us on the road."

Ian gave up that tack. He still felt an uneasiness, a foreboding.

"What do you think, Alison?" he asked.

"I don't know about you, my boy," said the hag, "but I shall keep my eyes peeled around this fellow!"

She took a small penknife from a pocket and made good her promise.

chapteR eiGht

One day, a beautiful princess sat upon a jewel-encrusted throne in a castle high atop a mountain. This was no ordinary castle, but a magical castle that seemed to be a craggy extension of the naked rock, its jagged towers caveless stalagmites without stalactites, its walls ragged upthrusts of obsidian. As to the exact nature of its magic, no one could say, but then everything was magical in the Dark Circle and so, presumably, was this castle. But the most curious aspect of this lofty stony perch in a land chock-full of curious structures was the virtual lack of staircases, ladders, elevators, pulleys, ski lifts, or any other kind of method to reach it where it perched atop sheer unclimbable cliffs.

But back to the princess.

Princess Alandra Bellworthy, to give her a name, although to be precise she was Queen Alandra Morgsteen, wife to the Dark Lord presently in vogue, Snirk Morgsteen. She was, however, a runaway wife, as she was happy to tell anyone who cared to ask, and tell at great length. But that was in the beginning of all this, and now Alandra was squarely in the middle of a great and majestic hall, with chandeliers and tapestries and lovely candles and torches and intricate carpets—indeed, the full panoply of majesty currently in style for medieval magical castles.

She was a spectacularly lovely woman, this princess, shining with youth and health through every pore of her creamy skin, through blue eyes and blond hair and large breasts and hips encased in satin, indeed all the dressings a human-type princess needed to excel in a land largely composed of fairies and the supernatural.

And what would a princess be without a court? All kinds of courtiers met her every need as she sat reading a book, a lovely golden cat lying peacefully in her lap. Truly, a beatific scene of serenity if ever there was one!

"Gods!" this perfect princess cried, slamming her volume closed and looking around her with indignation. "I am so bored!"

The startled cat screeched with fear and leaped to the top of the wooden throne, the hair on its back raised high. "The Norx!" the cat sobbed. "Have those awful Norx come to fetch us?"

"Narcs? Did you say narcs?" What had once appeared to be a nearby pile of rags grew legs and arms and wide, stoned eyes. "Wow, man. Bummer!" The skinny being skittered into the safety of a shadowed room, clutching a small plastic bag of weeds close to his chest.

"Why does that creature call itself a hippie?" Alandra wondered aloud. "It hasn't any hips to speak of at all!"

"Don't change the subject," said the cat called Alabaster, gazing furtively around the expanse of the great chamber. "I wanted to know if the Norx have found us yet."

"No, silly, of course not!" Alandra stood and placed her book—a Harold Robbins potboiler she'd found in Princerik's library—upon her plush cushion and began to pace. "That would be much too exciting for our host. The Norx can't get up and we can't get down! We're stuck, and I'm bored!"

The cat noticeably relaxed, then jumped down, curling lazily onto the cushion. "Well, don't look at me, oh Jewel Princess of the Rainbow! I'm supremely happy here, at least for the time being. Oh yes, I suppose that in, say, a year or so I shall want to start thinking about finding a way down to seek Crowley Nilrem, my master. But for now I am purrrfectly content and feeling purrrfectly safe within these walls, a touch weird and aerie though they be! Things have turned much too topsy-turvy of late. I need a safe and comfy place, and I have one, so why buck Fate when it tosses you in a luxurious lap?"

"Topsy-turvy!" Alandra cried, spinning around and fixing him with a cracked fingernail. "And whose fault is that, then? You claim you're the one who wrecked that Wraith Board! You're the one who caused everything to start collapsing!"

"I told you it wasn't my fault!" the cat returned defensively. "I was a mere pawn with paws! Some other force is at work in this matter, something deep and mysterious and primal." The cat licked the back of a leg once, twice, then yawned. "Now if you'll excuse me, since you're not making use of this cushion, I'll just take a nappie-poo."

A faint purple flush appeared on Alandra's cheeks. "You'll do nothing of the sort!" she cried, stalking forward and grabbing the cat by the skin at the back of his neck. She hoisted Alabaster and flung him across the room onto the table. Plates clattered, goblets fell. Wine spilled, fruit rolled. The cat skidded across the wood and slipped off the side. His front claws dug in and he hung on the edge, pure terror in his brown and green eyes. "Ye gods, you're a mean princess!" he gasped.

Alandra, immediately sorry, sped to his rescue. She lifted him and held him and cooed her apologies as she carried him back to the throne. "I am sorry, dear Alley Cat. I am spoiled, I admit, and I've a terrible temper. Forgive me."

"You're as difficult to live with as Crowley Nilrem!" the cat said, clinging to her silken sleeve, still terrified. "But yes, mistress, I forgive you. I've no choice in the matter!"

"Of course not, none at all! How can any creature do else but love me?" Alandra piped coquettishly, pleased with herself once more. "Am I not beautiful? Am I not charming?" Still clutching the golden cat, she twirled about, skirt and scarves swirling. "Oh, the suitors I had in my father's court. Oh, all the darling prancing boyfriends! The parties! The balls! And the dances were fairly wonderful as well."

She hummed a three-quarter-time tune and started to waltz.

"Mistress, please, I'm getting ... dizzy!" the cat moaned.

Alandra let her arms drop. "Oh, but I am so filled with ennui!"

The cat fell to the floor and scampered back up to the top of the throne for safety. "Things weren't so boring the first day you were here," said the cat, settling back into place but keeping an eye on her. "What with the spat with that hag! And humans think we fight noisily!"

A smug smile appeared on Alandra's face. "It

was a very simple case of the palace's being too small to hold the both of us. Clearly Princerik prefers my company and my kisses. Besides, she was just an old loony who had the dragoon flummoxed into thinking she was an appropriate lady of the house."

"Still, I'd watch out," suggested the cat. "She did promise to do a John the Baptist number on your head."

Alandra tilted her head inquiringly. "How so? I realize my messianic properties—I mean, my being the Key and all that—"

"No, no—head on a platter!" Alabaster illustrated by drawing a claw across his furry throat. "Lunchmeat!"

"Oh, Salome! Stuff and bother!" Alandra said, stamping a petite foot. "We'll have blown this joint by then. Surely my hero, Sir Godfrey, is on his way to rescue me!"

"Shhh!" said Alabaster. "We don't want Princerik to hear any of this. I certainly wouldn't mind getting out of this place either, I suppose. But I don't care to get booted into the Circle again from a great height. With my luck, I'd land on a Norx again!" The feline shuddered at the very thought.

"No, I don't blame you," said Alandra, continuing her pacing, barely noticing a pair of jesters frolicking at the other end of the hall, juggling skulls and bones. "But Alabaster, something must be done about my boredom, and done immediately. Won't you be a good cat and go look for Princerik? I haven't seen it all morning, and I should like to speak to it."

"Why me? You know that monster scares the fleas off me! I mean, it would if I had any!"

Alandra waved her hand in the air dismissively.

"Cats find things better. Everyone knows that! Besides, it's time to consult my runes. I shall address to them my problems of boredom and frustration."

"Oh, very well. Anything to prevent getting thrown across the room again!" He pounced upon the cushion, padded down onto the carpet, and slid across Alandra's shin with feline affection. "My goodness, red slippers—I don't suppose if you tapped them we'd head back to Kansas?"

"Don't be silly, Toto. I mean, Alabaster. This is reality! Now go find that damned dragoon."

"You love me, don't you, mistress?"

Alandra stooped and patted the cat atop his head. "Of course I love you, silly cat. Now do what I ask!"

A streak of gold and silver, the cat sped away across the room under the legs of a gigantic yellow bird pecking at sesame seeds, past a frog playing Parcheesi with a blue mop of a creature. Such boring beasts, Alandra thought, dismally shaking her head. All they seemed to want to do was to sing about numbers! Kid stuff!

She fell back into the cushions of her throne, which Princerik had dredged up from its basement ("Oh yes, I absolutely insist. Every princess must have a throne! If only to use to stand upon to give me a smooch!"), and she untied a pouch that dangled from her belt. She loosened the strings that cinched the top closed and peered into the darkness.

"Yoo hoo, stones. Time for a little rocking and rolling." She shook the felt pouch. It jangled satisfyingly, emitting the usual grunts and groans of waking sleepyheads. "I'm having problems here, runes. I know you've told me that I can expect to cool my heels awhile. But it's really getting to be just too much! Any divinations on the subject?"

She plucked one of the flat stones away from its fellows, immediately recognizing its markings as that of Orato, who often acted as spokesman for the group. She held it close to her ear.

"Really, your majesty," the rune piped in a clear, well-enunciated baritone. "You hardly give us any rest. The others are most unnerved. Our nerves are fraying! We were not created for adventures, and certainly not to be used so often. Why, I almost feel as though my markings were wearing away!"

"If you don't start cooperating, Orato," said Alandra, "I'll mark all your backs with X's and O's and play checkers with you!"

The stone sighed. "Very well, your majesty. What is it you wish?"

"I am bored, Orato. I wish to know how I can relieve the tedium."

"Yes, yes, quite apparent, your ladyship."

"Have you guys figured a way for me to get out of this place?" Alandra demanded.

"We have been searching the mystical currents, my lady, as promised. But there is still a great deal of confusion, and we can divine nothing." Suddenly, the pouch jerked, its stones clattering together noisily. "Oh dear, I believe they want to have a word with me. If you would, your ladyship . . ."

Alandra dumped Orato back in the bag and waited for the signal to pick him out again.

The Runes of Rachner had been the result of ten years of her Treasure Hunt—a program devised by her father's court of magicians to sharpen her abilities. From time to time, at various ages,

Alandra had been presented with riddles and maps and stories and such, which, once solved, led her to a new rune hidden or buried somewhere in her castle or its surrounding gardens and grounds. It had all been a grand game indeed, and Alandra was almost sorry when, at the age of fifteen, she had been informed that she'd found them all, and, with the correctly muttered spells from the magicians, they would turn into oracles, guiding her way through life. Often as not, she ignored their advice—but after her capture by the Dark Lord Snirk Morgsteen, she had come to rely on their rock-solid counseling. Solid, that is, until the wretched business of her botched escape.

Since then the stones, never totally on the ball personality-wise, had gotten weirder and weirder.

She listened to the stones until the jabbering stopped, then stuck her hand halfway into the bag. A stone leaped up and slid between her fingers. Orato.

"Milady!" said the runestone. "We have been reviewing the situation and the chaps would like some help in conjuring up a recollection from the recent past. Would you kindly hold the bag up near your left temple, close your eyes, and think back to when the dragoon carried you and your cat here?"

Alandra shrugged. "Certainly." There was nothing tedious about that time!

She did as directed, feeling the felt and the hardness beyond against her skin. Almost immediately, she felt her consciousness slipping away into a replay of time.

"Now remember when Princerik brought you here," Orato instructed.

And Alandra remembered.

*   *   *

"Don't drop me!" the cat cried, somehow digging his claws deeper into the torn fabric of Alandra's gown. "Oh, please don't drop me, mistress!"

Long leathery wings flapped overhead, as reality refocused around her. Strong limbs with hands half human and half talon clutched her fast against a large waistcoated chest. Eyes directed in the direction of its flight, the partially human face thrust out before them like the prow of some Viking ship, cutting through a misty northern sea.

With that vague, detached part of herself that watched all this instead of reexperiencing it, Alandra realized that the moment recalled was minutes after she and the cat had been snatched from the Norx guards, Toothmaw and Tombheart, assigned to carry her back to her husband Morgsteen in the kingdom of Blankshun. She heard her own voice say: "I know how you feel."

A deep voice rumbled from the thick body above them. "Do not be alarmed, oh princess. A virgin will come to no harm in these arms of mine," said the dragoon—half dragon, half goon. "And a cat of your name must be pure as well!"

"Oh hell!" whispered Alabaster. "We're in deep kitty litter."

Actually, they were high in the air, dancing with the clouds, and if Alandra had not been so terrified, she might have taken pleasure in the spectacular view afforded by the flight. The coils of what had once been the flat world of the Dark Circle and its environs stretched out below and above like a picture playfully scissored and strung up in a void of clouds and darkness. The dragoon appeared to be traversing a gap between sections of the coil; up ahead loomed a series of lopsided mountains, which slowly righted themselves as gravity magically adjusted to compensate.

Alandra closed her eyes, dizzy from the sensation, and the runes must have fast-forwarded the memory, because when she opened them again, what seemed like moments later, the summits of the range were much closer. Another jump-cut instant, and the dragoon was flying among the peaks so near sometimes that Alandra felt as though she could reach out and touch them.

"There it is, darling," said the dragoon. "Your new home." It released one of its limbs from Alandra and pointed ahead, allowing its passengers to slip somewhat. Cold wind beat in Alandra's face, and she screamed. "Oops," said the dragoon. "Oh dear, so sorry." It gathered them up again. "I grow excited with the nearness of my Keep."

Alandra's answering words could not get past her heart in her throat. The dragoon banked steeply and flapped toward the craggy manse at breakneck speed.

"Oh, I can't look!" cried Alabaster.

Alandra's eyes, though, seemed frozen open, and she watched as the precipitous walls grew closer and the dragoon dived down to land with a jarring abruptness. At that moment, two of Alandra's gown seams chose to tear. With a shriek, Alabaster tumbled the last four feet, landing on his paws. The terrorized feline tore across the courtyard to a door—but his escape was circumvented by a large form that suddenly filled the frame. With another, weaker cry, the cat about-faced and tore back into Alandra's arms. "Just in time, dear Alley Cat," she said, clutching the cat close to her chest. "My gown is torn and my modesty compromised."

The cat could not find his tongue, he seemed so agitated from his encounter with the creature in the doorway.

"Welcome, dear people, to Crag Keep," said Princerik the dragoon. "Do make yourselves at home. You will stay for a very long time, I should think, so you must feel yourselves a part of the family." It straightened its ruffled coat, from behind which its large wings sprouted. "Ah! I see we are being welcomed."

The form that had been lurking in the doorway detached itself from the shadows and walked out to them. Taller than a man, it was the ugliest woman that Alandra had ever seen.

"Alison, dear," said the dragoon, lightly brushing the dust of its travels from its shoulders. "Look who I have found! Another lovely woman to keep you company, and her cat as bonus."

"Lovely woman?" Alandra said. "I hope this doesn't shock you, Princey, but she looks to be a hag to me!"

The dragoon's eyes blinked. "Alison, dear, you never told me that. Is it true?"

The hag shuffled forward and thrust her blobby breasts into the dragoon's midriff. "Now, Princerik, honey, what's in a name?"

"A piece of dung by any other name would stink," murmured Alandra.

The hag shot Alandra a murderous glance. "And who is this, Princerik?" When Princerik explained, the hag began to complain shrilly. "Virgin princess for a companion? To kiss and keep? You rat! You two-timer! What do you need a virgin princess for when you have me?"

By this time, other denizens of the Keep had come out to watch. There were a pair of dwarves, an elf or two, a centaur, and several much smaller dragoons. All seemed fascinated by Alandra—they got as close to her as they dared.

"Am I giving off a scent?" Alandra whispered down to Alabaster.

"It must be your magic, mistress. Perhaps they've never seen a beautiful woman before."

Princerik and the hag bickered for a while, and finally the dragoon turned to Alandra. "Now, Alison, how do you expect me to give up this splendid bit of femininity? Surely you can accommodate her presence easily enough. You have had no problem with the other members of my family."

"Dammit, you need only one beautiful woman in your life!" cried Alison Gross. "And I'm her!" The hag squinted over at Alandra, her thick baggy nose twitching. "Besides, she smells of bad magic. Dangerous magic, I'm telling you." She clutched at her wobbly abdomen. "No wonder my innards are acting up. Because of that witch! I want her out, Princerik. Haul her pretty little tail out of my life!"

The bemused dragoon looked over to Alandra.

"Wonderful!" said Alandra. "Take me toward a place called Mullshire. I would hate to break up this happy home."

"Truly, dear lady, I cannot," returned the dragoon. "For you have captured my heart, and I would have you nearby always to nuzzle, to feel the rain of your kisses on these cheeks—"

The hag jumped up and down, screaming. "She'll be the death of you, Princerik. Don't you believe me? I can feel it in my gut!" She pulled open the bottom of her blouse and stuck her hand through. "Do you want to see?"

"My word," said Alabaster. "She's getting sickeningly literal, isn't she?"

The hag pulled out a length of intestine, to which was affixed a large tumorlike bulb, glowing with an unearthly light. Images began to flash within the bulb.

A voice sounded in Alandra's head: "Here we go—now you've got it, milady."

Suddenly, the memory slowed down to a crawl.

Orato's voice continued in her head. "Let's see if we can get a close-up on that Crystal Bowel. That's what we're after, milady. You take what you can get when it comes to prophecy."

As though her eyes had grown magnifying lenses, the Crystal Bowel suddenly occupied all of Alandra's vision. Orato was right—images could be seen through the glass contours. First, there was a confused sequence featuring Princerik and members of its family—including the hag, with some prominence. Then Alandra saw an oval mirror, with a frame of gold scroll in the rococo manner holding a reflection of—herself! This dissolved into an image of a group of knights traveling across a field. Her rescuers, surely, she thought, as she watched the image change to a scene depicting these same knights moving within the walls of this castle. And the handsome one . . . it must be none other than Godfrey Pinkham, her hero.

But wait . . . one of the others . . . no, it couldn't be!

It was.

It was the cripple who had blown her chances of escape!

Uh-oh.

Suddenly, the parade of images speeded up again. The voices resumed.

"You see, Princerik? This woman bodes no good. There are armed men who would do harm to get her back!" the hag insisted stridently.

"Aye, and armed Norx as well," returned the dragoon, "but surely you know, Alison, that this is no easy castle to storm! The mount and ramparts are steep, and I have quite suitable defenses. And just look at her!" A melting look appeared in the dragoon's eyes. "Is it not worth any strife to have her, for however short a time? No. She stays, and that is my final word on the matter."

"Either she goes or I go!" the hag screeched.

Not a bad idea, thought Alandra, and she sidled up to Princerik. "If the lady is to be unhappy at my presence here, my new love, then surely I will be unhappy as well!"

With a crash of wings and a scraping of ground, the dragoon was aloft. Claws dug into the hag's clothes, and she was yanked off the ground. "Come, Alison. It's time to visit your relatives far away in some dark wood."

"Princerik!" the hag shrieked in midair. "How could you?"

"Oh, I suspect you'll find your way back, lovey," returned the fading voice. "What you need, though, is some time to think."

"What about me?" Alandra yelled.

"My servants will show you to your quarters," returned the dragoon, flapping toward dusk, bearing its squawking burden.

"Okay!" said Orato. "That's quite enough, I believe."

The scene faded back to her throne chamber,

and Alandra found herself clutching the bag close to her face. "Milady, you see? You have rescuers coming. All you must do is be patient."

"That mirror," said Alandra in a quiet voice. "What is the meaning of that mirror?"

"Mirror? Oh—surely it was something the hag valued . . . some image she was—digesting." The rune chuckled at its own joke.

"Something she owned!" crowed Alandra. "And it was beautiful. And I must have it! Oh, runes, you have solved my problem. What better way to relieve the tedium than to go on a Treasure Hunt? And that is just want I intend to do!"

Alabaster chose that fortuitous moment to reappear, scampering along the littered floor, then leaping into the princess's lap. "I found him, mistress," the cat said breathlessly. "He approaches! Oh, a tidbit in reward!" Alabaster yeaked delightedly. He snatched the stone and gulped it whole.

"Alley! That was one of my runes!"

"Oh, sorry. I confess, it does feel a bit heavy in my stomach."

A tiny outraged voice could be heard from inside the cat. The runes in the sack clattered with upset at the fate of their companion.

Alabaster lifted his right leg and addressed his abdomen. "Don't worry, friend. I've been working on a hairball for a while. Just hang on and I'll get you back."

"Somewhere other than in my lap, please?" Alandra said, disgustedly pushing the cat away. She looked up and saw Princerik entering the chamber.

All the rooms, halls, and doorways of the Keep were spaciously designed so that the dragoon could

navigate and occupy them easily. Still, the creature had to fold its wings in somewhat so that it
could slip through the portal. Alabaster had apparently interrupted it in its study, because the
dragoon was wearing a long flowing dressing gown
of red-and-blue Chinese silk and smoking a long
curving pipe. Half-frame spectacles were propped
above a stubby nose. The dragoon puffed a burst
of smoke as it approached the throne, then removed its pipe.

"Yes, my dear?" it said. "Your familiar requested
my presence. You are bored? Do you seek relief
by kissing me, you insatiable female?" The dragoon chuckled good-humoredly, with great self-
satisfaction. "You should be lucky I'm not the
type of dragon who eats princesses. Much better
to cherish them lingeringly, I say!"

Alandra finished fastening her rune bag back to
her belt, then rose and sauntered slinkily to her
captor, being sure one of her shoulders was exposed. She slipped her hand through the silk
dressing gown and began to rub its greenish lizard-
skin belly. The dragoon virtually cooed with
contentment.

"Princey-poo," she said in a little-girl voice. "I
was indeed bored, but I have discovered a distraction. Tell me where your friend Alison Gross
stayed in this Keep."

"Hmm? Alison? Why do you want to know
about her? You needn't be jealous."

"Oh, I know. Now lean over and let these hun-
gering lips touch your quivering cheek!" The
dragoon obeyed, and Alandra gave it a wet smacking kiss. Its skin was bitter-tasting, salty, but not
entirely unpleasant. As usual, the dragoon's eyes
began to roll deliriously. Its breaths came faster.

"I should like to explore the hag's quarters, Princerik," said Alandra. "You don't mind, do you?"

"Mind? No, of course not."

Alandra kissed him again. "So where are they?"

Blissed out, the smiling dragoon shrugged. "I don't know. Now how about the other cheek, my love?"

"You don't know!" Alandra said.

"This is a large place, and it has been in my family a very long time! There are tunnels and steps that go down deep into the heart of the mountain. When I collected Alison, I told her, as I told you, to find anywhere she pleased to reside. She mentioned that she had found quite suitable quarters some ways down! Where exactly that place is, I can't say."

Alandra contained her frustration. "But you will allow me to search for this place, will you not?" She planted a long one on the other side of the ugly reptilian face.

"Yes, of course, though do promise not to spend too long, or I shall have to send servants to fetch you," said the dragoon, clearly pleased with its decision. "Yes, I should think that there are many sights below that will relieve your boredom—and perhaps make you happy in your safe and comfortable place up here with me."

Alandra threw her arms as far as they could go around its neck. "Oh, thank you, Princerik." She gave it two quick smooches. "And I promise you more of the same when I get back!"

The dragoon, a lovelorn look on its face, wandered dreamily back to its study as Alandra raced over to where Alabaster had just managed to upchuck his hairball and Orato.

Happily, she picked up the rune, wiped it on the rug, and dropped it back into her sack with its fellows to recuperate from the ordeal.

"Well now, darling kitty. Do you feel like a little exploring?"

"I really would prefer to take a nap, mistress."

"Oh, come now. Cats are supposed to be curious! While we wait for our rescuers, we shall find the hag's room, and I shall have that wonderful mirror!" She rubbed her hands together. "A Treasure Hunt!" She patted her felt bag. "What do you say to that, runes?"

A tiny voice yelped through the bag: "Just keep us away from that cat!"

chapter nine

the cottage that Mr. Erasmus Trollkein had promised proved to be closer to barn status. True, Ian observed, it had the essential cottage ingredients—namely saggy wattle-and-daub roof, chimney pots, quaint stone walls, and a cute wooden door in the center like a round mouth to the eyes of the windows. But it was hardly of cottage proportions to Ian's judgment. It was more on the scale of a—

"Trolling Alley!" announced Erasmus Trollkein, proudly brandishing his shiny walking stick toward his home. "Named after a cherished tradition of my much-missed home world."

"Oh, you are not of this planet, sir?" said Sir Oscar Cornwall, who, Ian had noticed, seemed to keep his oculars on the occult most, and was doubtless the most knowledgeable in such matters.

"No, I am from my mother's world untimely ripped," said the troll with a sigh. "But let us not dwell on unhappy stories, gentlemen. We have reached my abode. Did you know that if a home is a castle, it's a hassle? That's why I much prefer the comforts of cottage life. Yes, a hearth, a glass of port, a good woman, a good book, and what more can a troll ask for?''

Their detour had been a little farther off their path than the troll had indicated, but then it was most likely closer in troll measure of distance. Erasmus had apologized that he did not have a trolley to carry them in (at which he giggled weirdly), but by that time so many sugarplums and the like were dancing in the heads of the knights that they most likely would not have minded twice the distance.

His question being purely rhetorical, the troll had proceeded to stride forward, leading them to the rounded doorway. He wiped his boots and invited the knights to tie up their horses in the bushes, saying he would bring them some feed and apple cores for their own feast later on.

"Now just a moment, my new friends," he said, opening the door and peering into the gloom within. "Let me go in first and warn Mrs. Trollkein that we have company. The dear lady takes badly to abrupt surprises of this nature, even though she absolutely craves guests!" With that said, he eased his bulk into the shadows and was gone.

"I don't want to go in," Ian said, backing away.

"Oh, Ian," said Hillary. "Really. You are just not a good judge of character. A milder person I've never seen before in my life!"

"Look, Ian, dear boy," said Godfrey Pinkham in his smooth familiar voice. "We've still got our weapons hanging at our sides! We've still got our wits and our strength! Prick up your self-confidence, lad! *Carpe diem!* Seize the day!"

Ian was more worried about seizures, actually, he was so jittery about this whole business. How could these knights be so calm about entering the den of monsters, even if it was to have tea? Self-confidence, hell ... self-preservation was higher up on Ian Farthing's list! Still, perhaps they were right. He had to muster up courage ... and going for tea with trolls was as good a time as any for that!

Sharp-pitched voices drifted out for a moment. A clatter of pots and pans, thumps, and then silence. Within a moment, Erasmus Trollkein returned, carrying a large candle and looking slightly more rumpled and disheveled. "I'm afraid that the missus was initially not very happy with word of company, but when she learned that you are questers, her entire attitude changed! So come, come and forgive this dark corridor, and watch your step! The next room is much better lit!"

With jingle of chain mail and jangle of spur, the knightly company followed.

The thick-wicked candle was almost torchlike, illuminating framed pictures on the wall, some depicting trolls, but most quite complex scenes of saints, crucifixions, and suchlike.

"Don't ask me what these be, friends," said Erasmus Trollkein, noting the glances of the knights. "The missus and I just hung them up for decoration. Found them fallen hither and yon across the landscape. Regular rain of stuff sometimes, when the weather acts up. Sometimes come a bit damp, but dried out, they make good firewood, if we don't like 'em. Just other day, this awful painting of a smiling woman labeled *Moaner Liza* or something proved to be excellent kindling."

The troll blew out his candle. "Next room's a bit better."

The foyer gave way to a chamber with windows providing light. The room was piled with all kinds of junk and knickknacks and what-have-yous. A shelf was full of dozens of odd toys. A pinball machine squatted in the corner beside a broken video game. Stuffed animals abounded, along with stacked items of furniture, busts, and a pair of television sets.

"Please don't ask me what all this stuff is," the troll explained. "I just find it spread hither and thither in the valley, and what I take a fancy to, I collect. But you've no time to dawdle, so just follow me!"

Ian was tempted to reach out and touch something. What a collection! But he kept his hands to himself as the group single-filed into a large room with cabinets and sinks and stoves and ovens and a female troll, all quite outsized, clearly the kitchen variety.

"Here they are, my dear, just as I promised!" said Erasmus Trollkein. "Gentle people, allow me to introduce you to my very own trollop! My wife, Abigail Troll!!"

She was only perhaps a foot shorter than hubby, but if anything she was more grotesque, rivaling even Alison Gross for facial deformity. A long bent nose snaked out from a pitted and hairy face, upon which spectacles perched precariously. Her chin seemed a younger sister to the nose, jutting absurdly out amid cheeks puffed as though with perpetual blowing. Her black-and-gray hair was, if anything, rattier than Mr. Troll's, and Ian was astonished to see that it actually had a bird's nest buried in it, complete with robin, content-edly munching fleas and lice from the hair. Otherwise, the troll, like her counterpart, was quite

respectably dressed in neatly pressed skirt and
blouse. An apron embroidered with a pair of hearts
pierced by a fishhook and labeled "Trolling for
Love" finished this distorted picture of a complete homebody.

"Well now," she said in a basso profundo that
curled the ample hairs on Ian Farthing's toes.
"What have we here!"

"Questers, my love, as promised," replied her
lesser half.

"Best questers in the business, at your service,
madam!" Sir Godfrey said, bowing. Then he
pointed to Ian Farthing. "The gesture is to our
jester quester, Master Ian Farthing." One by one,
Godfrey ticked off the company's names. "And
last and best, madam," he finished, "myself, Sir
Godfrey Pinkham, at your service."

"Have a seat at the table, then, and we'll have
your tea for ye soon!"

The table was quite large, and as there were
limited chairs, the knights found themselves shar-
ing the chairs, table top at nose level.

"Right then. Comfortable?" asked Erasmus as
he helped his wife by slicing up an absolutely
mammoth rum cake.

The knights replied that they were. " 'ere," said
Ronald Komquatte. "You mentioned summat 'bout
applejack. I confess, I have a bit of a thirst!"

"Oh yes, and all other sorts of drinks, gentlemen," returned the troll, immediately abandon-
ing his task and trotting to a cabinet, his steps
thunderous. The cabinet proved to contain dozens of bottles with various labels, including Jack
Daniel's, Dewar's, and Johnny Walker. Glass
clanked as the troll held up a number of the

bottles between his fingers. "I find these lovelies from time to time in the fields yonder in the early mornings. Mountain dew if ever I saw it, eh? Strong stuff!" When he met blank looks, he put the bottles back. "Well, I suppose you lads would prefer something more familiar, eh? The jack's outside. I'll just be a moment."

Hanging cutlery rattled as the troll stomped out another door, leaving the company alone with his wife. Mrs. Trollkein, having finished slicing the cake but neglecting as yet to serve it, busied herself at another table, laying pie dough down in pans. No sign, however, could be seen of what would be the contents of the pie.

"Air pie, Mrs. Trollkein?" asked Godfrey Pinkham in a good-natured manner.

"Nay, there be somethin' in it soon enough," the lady troll rumbled. "The oven must heat up and the dough must sit awhile."

"Alas, we can only stay for a short time."

"A pity!" the trollop said, then hunkered back to a surly silence.

"Ah, the joys of married life," grumped Sir William, trying to get his burly self comfortable in the mammoth chair he shared with Sir Stephen Jentile. "Reminds me of the wife at home. And you wondered why I was so eager to leave, Pinkham!"

A teapot started whistling stridently, and Mrs. Troll traipsed over loudly to the stove to attend to it. Ian, in his place beside Hillary atop another chair, watched Sir William's deep-set eyes follow her suspiciously. "Aye, she's a right one, Pinkham, and I don't know if I like the lay of this land!"

"You like it not at troll, eh, Mac?" said Godfrey

Pinkham, mimicking the squat knight's gruff voice. "Well, let me tell you, lads, I happen to have a reason for accepting this invitation," he whispered as the lady troll clinked and crashed among teacups and saucers and such. "I've heard my fairy stories of the Dark Circle," he continued, whispering. "And this house verifies the fact that trolls are packrats!"

"Treasure!" cried Mortimer Shieldson. "Of course! We steal their bloody treasure!" His droopy eyes opened wide, glinting almost metallically with the prospect.

"No, no, simpleton!" Sir Godfrey said, slapping him atop the head with a loose gauntlet. "There'll be treasure aplenty at the end of the quest." He leaned over toward Alison Gross. "Is it not true, hag, that trolls are known to hoard interesting and useful items such as magical rings, talismans, enchanted swords, and such that might be of wondrous value in our mission?"

"Oh yes, they are notorious for their ability in findin' goodies like those," said Alison, nodding her head briskly, letting loose a rain of dandruff.

"But however do you intend to pry loose any one of these things, Godfrey?" Hillary Muffin declared.

"You shall see, dear girl," said Godfrey cagily. "Ah, but here comes our host."

Indeed, Ian saw, the troll was lumbering in, arms wrapped around a large ceramic jug, which he thunked onto a counter. "Here we go, gentle people. Now, I believe you have some very splendid goblets placed before you. If you'll just come forward, I'll fill you up."

"You first, Ian," urged Godfrey. "Have a good stiff drink. You need it most."

Ian admitted to himself that perhaps for once Godfrey Pinkham was not only right, but speaking for Ian's best interest here. A regular imbiber of ale, Ian missed his daily two pints and could use some applejack, especially now, what with all he'd been through and his present nervous disposition.

There was in fact a goblet before him, a silvery goblet, embedded with designs. It was large and heavy, but Ian had discovered to his gratification that his strength had increased slightly with each day inside the Circle, and he could carry the thing. He toted it over to the troll, who, closer up, seemed an even jollier sort.

"Well then, me lad, a chap after mine own heart. Such generous companions you have to let you go first! Put your vessel up." Ian obeyed and was rewarded by a healthy splash of sweet-smelling liquid. It was amber-colored, rich and frothy. "Well, then, me handsome lad! Drink hearty and tell them what a fine drink this is!"

Ian needed no encouragement. He grasped the cup firmly by one end, fitted the cold metal to his lips, and tilted. The stuff rolled coolly, nectar-delicious, down his throat, and it was so light and frothy it seemed as though he gulped for a very long time. He had to come up for air, though, and when he did, he smacked his lips with satisfaction, already feeling a tingling rush in his head, a suffusing warmth all through his body.

He smiled over to the knights and was about to pronounce the applejack good when he noticed how intently they were watching him, particularly Sir Godfrey.

He realized why they had had him taste first, and almost gagged at the thought of his stupidity.

He'd been their taster! They'd let him have first go to see if the stuff was poison.

"You bastards!" he spluttered.

"Pardon me?" asked Erasmus Trollkein.

Godfrey sprang up and patted Ian on the back. "There, there, Master Farthing, you shouldn't gulp your brew!" The knight smiled up at the troll. "He said, 'That stuff's hard!' "

"Well, of course it's hard. It's hard cider," chuckled the troll.

Ian took a couple of maddened swings at Godfrey, but the taller man warded them off by keeping him at arm's length. "Playful chap, Ian," the knight explained to Erasmus. "Always wants to play tag."

"Ho, ho!" said the troll. "Well, if you don't come to me, I'll come to you. Here, good knights," he said, moving to the table and beginning to splash out healthy dollops of applejack. "Drink hearty! To your health!"

"Health indeed!" cried Sir Godfrey, grabbing hold of Ian and examining him for signs of poisoning and finding none. "Master Farthing here seems to have had a great benefit of health!"

Hillary Muffin, already by Ian's side and coming to the same conclusion, kicked Godfrey in the shin nonetheless. "You're a rotter, you are, Pinkham!"

"Yeouch," said Godfrey, and he let Ian go. As Ian had already surmised that he was not poisoned, but in fact feeling quite excellent, he let bygones be bygones, picked up his fallen goblet, and hurried over to get another spill of drink.

"For pitcher or pourer, eh, lad?" squeaked the troll in his silly voice.

Hillary hurried away from possible reprisal from Godfrey, who almost pursued but thought better to drown his pain in a cup of the applejack. In fact, the entire scene turned from relatively sedate to decidedly raucous, the knights taking advantage of the huge goblets to drink huge amounts of the applejack and then squabbling among themselves about who was to get the next refill. Erasmus Trollkein cheerfully obliged with the help of his seemingly bottomless jug. Even Alison Gross joined in, slurping and cackling with glee, any uneasiness apparently allayed.

In the midst of this, Ian Farthing suddenly slapped his hands to his stomach. Gurgling and wretching, he fell to the wood floor and began to squirm piteously about.

The knights stopped their revelry and stared down in horror at their fallen companion, then blinked at their drinks.

Ian stopped moving with one spastic twitch . . .

. . . and then started tittering with laughter as he bounded to his feet and wobbled to the troll, holding forth his goblet for more.

Everyone laughed, even the troll, and jollity commenced again.

Only Hillary abstained, looking upon all of the spillage and slurping, biliousness and burping, with disdain. "Mr. Trollkein, really, I thought we were going to have tea!" she called out over the hubbub. "Tea and cakes!"

Erasmus Troll had by now poured and quaffed his own bucket-sized cup, and his hazy eyes signified that he was rapidly joining into the spirit of the festivities. "Oh, yes, yes! Abigail, serve the young miss the tea and bring the cakes around."

The troll put to rest any lingering doubts about poison by cramming a handful of cake into his maw and following it with tea when it came round.

The knights eagerly set to the supply of the cake.

"Delicious!" Ian cried, finding the cake almost as intoxicating as the applejack. "However did you make this?"

"The missus experiments," explained Erasmus. "This is rum cake, made from bottles of the stuff we've collected." He turned to his wife. "You've a smashing success, lovey! Everyone adores the stuff!"

For the first time, Mrs. Trollkein grinned, showing teeth just as clean and white and pointy as her husband's. She went back to her work on her pies, humming to herself like a sick bassoon.

Ian felt positively terrific, the best he'd felt in a very long time. Perhaps, he thought to himself as he drank some more of the cider, we could convince Mr. Erasmus Trollkein to part with a keg of this stuff and I can stay permanently snookered the rest of the journey. Yes, now that would be a treasure indeed!

Godfrey Pinkham, however, after making sure that he personally topped the troll's goblet twice (the jug had lessened in weight by a very great deal) and the troll was lolling happily in his chair, massive stomach gurgling and chortling with gastronomic glee, changed the subject from general barroom banter to the matter of magical devices.

"Dear Mr. Trollkein, we are overwhelmed by your hospitality!" the knight avowed in a trilling tenor.

The troll nodded, and bobbed his head in happy acceptance of the thanks. "As I say, the missus and I love to taste . . . er, toast healthy questers!" He held up a weaving goblet and then quaffed the contents.

Hastily, Sir Godfrey personally filled the vessel again from the diminishing jug. "Yes, and I can speak for us all when I tell you that we are absolutely astonished at all of the wondrous items you have collected!" He waved an alluding hand wildly over his head. "Why, there must be unimaginable treasures stored here in this humble but happy abode!"

"Oh, this and that," said the troll, a sly smile creeping over his face.

"We must confess that this company is fairly ignorant of things magical," Godfrey continued. "And yet now we find ourselves in an ensorceled existence. I thought, Mr. Erasmus Trollkein, that perchance you might have some magical items to show us and thus perhaps educate us better in the workings of such matters."

Erasmus Trollkein blinked, clearly slightly bemused at the question. "Now that you mention it, I do happen to have a cache of items I've found in my scavenging hereabouts. But truth to tell, I'm not quite sure what exactly they are, so it's hard to say if they are magical or no!"

"If it is not any trouble, perhaps you might allow us to have a look at these things, and we can help you determine their worth!" suggested Godfrey. "Who knows, we may all be educated in the effort."

"Why not?" said the troll, almost to himself. "What harm? Stay there. I shall fetch my cache and we shall see what we shall see."

He eased himself heavily from his chair and lumbered from the room.

Ian, resting his mouth awhile from imbibing, wandered innocently over to where Mrs. Trollkein was busy starting to cut up vegetables for her pies.

The trollop wielded her huge carving knife with practiced ease, slicing up carrots and potatoes, onions and beans, then methodically placing them in the bottom of the first deep-panned pie. She was so immersed in her task she did not seem to notice Ian's presence and she sang a little song to herself:

> "Fee fie foe fum,
>   Questing pie tonight,
>   Yum, Yum!"

Woozily, Ian moved closer and stared down into the pie pan to see if there was anything else within the crust. No rabbit, no quail or any other kind of element. What kind of pie was this, then?

"A vegetable pie, Mrs. Trollkein?" he asked, for the cake had been scrumptious and he absently thought he might get recipe hints from this otherwise unproductive quest. "I have never heard of that!"

Startled, she jumped, and her carving knife slammed down upon the cutting board, chopping five cabbages in half.

"You scrawny little runt!" she boomed. "Whatever do you want, poking your nostrils into trollish concerns? It will be nose pie if you don't remove your filthy self from here!"

Ian defensively clutched his nose and staggered

backward, confused. "Mr. Trollkein assured us that you loved questers!"

Her ugly face calmed a bit and assumed a faint smile. A bumpy tongue described the length of a lip, licking. "I do, scrawny one, when they keeps their places. Now begone and enjoy our hospitality and don't meddle!"

Ian, unsettled by this behavior but suspicion insulated by the large amount of alcohol running rampant in his veins, retreated, noting gladly that the much more affable member of the pair was returning with his treasure and a jolly smile. He easily carried a chest that two men might have difficulty with, grasping it by both handles.

"No, my friends, I have little truck with magic, though as I say I am a collector, and naturally when something interesting, magical or not, falls into my hands, I keep it," he said, setting the chest down and brushing off some of the dust and cobwebs with a humongous handkerchief. "Like a few years ago, a couple of questing hoboes wandered by—"

"Hobbits, dear," corrected his wife, peeling a potato with practiced dexterity.

"Right. Name of Bilbous and Frog, I think. Well, they left behind some stuff . . . a very nice ring, for instance, though it's of no use to me whatsoever since I can't fit it on, not even on my pinky!"

"They were very good!" Mrs. Trollkein said, her stomach rumbling like contained thunder as she leaned over her work again.

"Had a whopper of a story, I must say! You know, with all the stories I've heard, I might just put them down on paper, becoming a best-selling author on some world, eh? J. Growl Trollkein. Has a certain ring to it, eh?"

"I'm afraid, Mr. Trollkein," said Godfrey, barely containing his patience, "that we've much more interest in magic rings and saving princesses than we do in your literary endeavors."

The troll raised his bushy eyebrows. "Oh. Oh dear me, of course, but I do ramble on much too much. You want to see what we have in here that might help you find this Alandra lady and put things back to rights." He fumbled in his jacket pockets for his keys to deal with the padlock that hung on the chest. "This might take a minute. Have another drink while you wait!"

The knights did not need a second invitation to help themselves to more from the considerably lightened cask while the troll's keys jangled against the lock.

With a squeak of hinges, the lid of the chest opened. Brilliant rays of light streaked outward, and a momentary dust of dazzles sprinkled to the floor.

Trollkein squinted as he stuck his hand into the cache. "You know, I really can do without these magical special effects," he said, scooping up some of the contents.

The knights pressed in closer to see. Ian craned his neck to get a gander. Even Hillary, before now aloof from the proceedings, seemed to be fascinated by the cascade of colors from the box.

A scent of old cedar filled the room as Trollkein stirred his hand through the contents of the box. Diamonds and coins and rings dribbled between his fingers, a technicolor waterfall. The mouths of the knights dropped open as the glitter reflected in their eyes, seeming to throw back the dreams of avarice in their minds.

"And this is magical too?" said Godfrey, reaching out with his hand.

The troll deflected his reach. "I should be careful here, Sir Godfrey. You never know about magic things. You might get a terrible rash if you reach in too quickly. And, of course, I should prefer to keep the pretty stuff. Does my heart good to see a gem twinkle. Now, as to what might be of benefit for your quest . . ."

Metal clinked and stones clattered as the troll pulled out a small hibachi. "Oh yes. This does wonders for a quick campfire dinner. The Holy Grill. Cooks up hot dogs with that special saintly tang."

"Actually no," said Godfrey. "We were looking for something, well, a little more profound."

"Hmmm. Well, we've got manic mandalas, nervous necklaces, packs of cards, etc., etc. Remind me again just what exactly you had in mind."

"How about weapons effective in liberating princesses?" suggested Godfrey.

" 'ere!" cried one of the knights. "The boys and I will take a few baubles, too!"

"Shut up!" cried Godfrey. "Didn't you hear me? We'll get our treasures later once we've rescued Alandra!"

"Store your treasure in Heaven and not on earth!" intoned Hillary didactically.

"Say!" said Trollkein, pulling up something long and heavy. "What have we here?"

Ian saw that it was a morningstar, a long macelike affair with a deadly cluster of points at its top. Only the most expert of knights used them in the tournament games, since they were quite dangerous.

"A magic weapon?" Godfrey said eagerly. "What are its special qualities?" Ian watched his face assume a kind of dopey aspect, a yearning quality which somehow made the preening fellow look less lofty and yet more ridiculous.

"Hmm," said Trollkein. "There appears to be some sort of runic writing along the handle. Perhaps that might give us a hint, eh?" He pushed up from his crouch beside the chest and pulled out a pair of half-frames, which he slid over his big nose. "There now, what have we here? 'This be a special weapon for the killing of'—my goodness, I can't quite make out that next word."

Sir Ronald Komquatte waved his hand excitedly. "I know a little runic! Let me have a go!"

"Why certainly!" The troll lowered the weapon so that the man could see it.

Sir Ronald Komquatte, a bit bowlegged from a lifetime of riding horses, rambled over with a self-satisfied smile and squinted at the thick handle. " 'This be a weapon especially employable in the killing of . . . of . . .' " His eyes shot open, his mouth dropped, and he started trembling even as his hand reached for the hilt of his sword.

A gleam of excited satisfaction in his eye, Trollkein brought the morningstar down quickly and unmercifully upon the knight's head, smashing it like a ripe pumpkin.

The drunken questers watched flabbergasted as their colleague toppled to the floor with barely a twitch or other kind of complaint. Mrs. Trollkein, pure delight on her face, bounded up and snatched the freshly killed man, pulled him into her kitchen like a spider its prey, and began hacking him into pieces.

"Questing pie!" she cried. "My favorite!"

Somewhat sobered by the sight, the knights immediately scrabbled for their swords. Ian Farthing, however, immediately scrabbled for the door.

Halfway there, the ruckus of metal on sheaths, metal on metal filling the air, he was tackled soundly. He slammed to the floor, groaning. "Don't put me in the pie," he cried, feeling one of his fits imminent. "I don't like pie!"

"Ian Farthing!" Hillary cried amid the hubbub. "You have a sword, too! Don't desert us! Don't desert me!"

Ian looked up at his friend and was immediately ashamed. The emotion drove away some of his panic, and he remembered how he had failed Alandra and how that failure had caused this entire mess in the first place. Cowardice in him seemed so automatic. Yet there was more, much more, to Ian, and he had proved that. So why was he running away?

To save his skin, that was why. These trolls were huge.

Trollkein stood before the confused collection of besotted knights holding his morningstar like a maestro before an orchestra about to direct a cacophonic symphony. He looked unruffled by his kill, though with his mouth open now, the length and sharpness of his teeth were pronounced, and his entire aspect was much more fearsome, despite his gentleman's attire.

The knights, however, stomachs full of drink, were a mess, stumbling and bumbling about, bumping into each other as they prepared a battle stance against their newly realized enemy.

It looked bad, and Ian turned again to run.

But his way was blocked by Alison Gross, recovered from her shock, who had the same idea.

He struck her and rebounded, held from toppling
by Hillary. The sight of the hag's bloated, ratty form
bounding away, her wretched face a travesty of
self-preservation, sent a cold shock down Ian's
backbone. She looked like an oversized parody of
himself.

He turned to Hillary, who stared at him implor-
ingly, and said, "You're right."

He reached into his pocket for the Pen—but his
hand closed upon empty air.

Meanwhile, under the shouted orders of Sir
Godfrey, the crew of remaining knights managed
to get themselves into a semblance of order, their
swords bristling out like spines on some monstrous sea urchin.

"Hold, troll!" cried Godfrey. "Desist or die!"

Trollkein grinned and chuckled at this.

"Wait!" said Sir Stephen Jentile. "I have an
idea! We shall take his wife hostage!" He took a
step toward the trollop.

Mrs. Trollkein looked up from her grisly task.
She raised her gigantic carving knife, glistening
with blood, and brandished it. "Just try it, fellows!"

Sir Stephen backed away hastily to join his
fellows, but tripped over the leg of a fallen chair,
stumbled out toward the hulking troll, and sprawled
face flat before him, like a knightly offering.

Before the knight could scramble away, a meaty
hand descended and pinned him to the floor. A
boot kicked the knight's sword from his hand.
"Well now, another visitor come to read the rest
of the runes?" the troll said. "Perhaps you'll find
them to be a recipe for knight pie!"

Sir Stephen Jentile squawked and floundered
as the troll picked up the knight with one hand
and let him dangle.

"So then!" cried Sir Godfrey, recovering his powers of rhetoric. "This is your hospitality?" he blustered.

"I am always hospitable to my wife," said Trollkein, "and I always bring her home what she likes in her pies. And this time, I have struck"—he brought the morningstar hard against Sir Stephen's noggin—"one of her favorites." He tossed the lifeless body over to his wife, who proceeded delightedly to dress it for another pie.

After watching in a trance of horror, Godfrey cried, "You can't get away with this! We are questers on holy business!"

"Well then, come, come and have your vengeance," said Trollkein, grinning obscenely and beckoning with his bloodied morningstar. "And I shall broil you on my Holy Grill in personal memory of the mission of your quest." Trollkein leered evilly. "Oh yes, you knights on holy quests are such a trip! Full of yourselves, convinced that God is on your side. I suppose that's why the missus and I always find your ilk tasty—perhaps it's the pride and bravado that run through your sinews that make them so delicious. Also, this way we can digest your stories before we digest you!" A drop of spittle dripped from the side of the troll's mouth in anticipation of the feast before him. "Thus, a double profit." The thing—more bestial at every moment—took a step toward the knights.

"Wait!" cried Sir Godfrey desperately. "Be warned! We have a secret weapon!" The leader of the group looked behind him and espied Ian Farthing, searching his pockets. He reached back and tugged Ian forward, whispering in his ear, "There's a good lad, do your stuff!" He propelled the smaller fellow toward the troll.

Ian gazed up at this imposing mountain of flesh and muscle before him and found it difficult to control his bladder.

Trollkein looked down his ponderous belly at the bedraggled and bent human being and laughed a squeaky laugh. "A secret weapon! The notion is worthy of inclusion in one of my stories! But are you the secret weapon, Master Farthing, or is it some item on your apparel?"

"The latter, sir, and if you'll let me find it, I shall show it to you!" Ian exclaimed tremulously.

Then he remembered. Of course! For safekeeping, he had used his cobbling skills and fashioned a carrier for the pen in his boot. The drink in him must have made him forget! He reached down and pulled the thing out: a tapered cylinder with a steel button and clip at the top. Funny, thought Ian, it felt different now, tingly where the cool metal connected with his fingertips. There seemed to be somewhat of a nimbus about it as well.

"My goodness, I've seen those things in my collecting," said the troll. "I believe it is called a ball-point pen and it is used for writing. What, do you intend to write me to death? Come, come, lad, give it here and I'll make speedy and painless work of you, though I must say you don't look as though you've much meat on those bones." The troll advanced, raising his morningstar.

"Come on, Ian!" cried Godfrey. "There's a good lad! You did it with Kogar and you did it with that hand!"

Ian touched the button.

There was a click.

But instead of a rapierlike length of metal growing from the end of the pen, this time the light nimbus sparkled brighter, growing out into a long flat blade, with a hilt. And the rainbow of sparkle did not stop there but glittered up the length of his arms, turning them from thin limbs into bare bands of thickly corded muscle.

Ian wasn't sure what to do.

The troll blinked and staggered back a bit with shock. "The Pen That Is Mightier Than the Sword! The Metaphor Made Metal!" The ugly face rested in thought for a moment, and the troll lowered his morningstar.

"Right!" he said, suddenly all smiles. "I believe we've enough questers for a fine pair of pies, my love!" He turned to the others and said, "So, gentlemen, you may depart with your lives and my blessings. Now, if you'll excuse me, I should like to get to my study and jot down some notes on the most interesting things you've told me!"

"Just a minute!" said Ian. "You can't . . . can't just kill two people, put them in a pie, and get away with it!"

The other knights grunted their approval of this situation.

Trollkein sighed wearily and turned back to face his guests. "Now, dear chaps, you must admit that my wife and I are quite a lot larger and more powerful than you. I hold in my hands a magical weapon, and you, Ian Farthing, hold in your hands a magical weapon, which does indeed even things up a tad. In other words, someone other than you folks might get hurt, and the possibility annoys me. As I said, two knights are quite sufficient to our needs. You can't bring them back to life—so just be happy to leave with yours, eh?"

A light flashed in his eyes. "I'll tell you what!" He looked over to the chest of magical items. "You gentlemen seemed quite interested in this collection of goodies here. Let's not have your visit to the Trollkein home entirely a bad memory. Perhaps a little remuneration will help." His bushy eyebrows rose suggestively. "Go your way now, and I shall give you a few of these magical trinkets. With a few gems and coins to sweeten the load, eh? Mrs. T., be a good trollop and bring over that rucksack and we'll load it up with goodies for these excellent knights so that they can be on their way!"

Mrs. Troll obediently brought the sack over, eyeing Ian and his sword-pen with a wary frown.

As for Ian, he stood there feeling a number of emotions. Shock and surprise, certainly, but also a numbness. And below the numbness, a power. He wondered if he should do something in the way of retribution for his fellow knights' deaths—but something, be it caution or just plain fear, kept him standing in place.

"Yes, you see," Godfrey spoke up pompously. "There you have it. That sword could rip the rolls right out of you trolls. But perhaps you are right, Trollkein. There could be a tussle, and I should not like to lose any more knights. Although be aware there is no doubt that we could leave you stewing in your own pies, you disgraceful swine!"

"But everyone has a few bad habits!" Trollkein

protested, pouting as he dropped assorted stuff into the thick burlap bag.

Ian felt pretty silly standing with a pair of arms that would look more at home on a bronze statue of a hero, holding a sword that normally he'd be incapable of lifting. Still, he didn't particularly care to use it, though it seemed to put the fear of God in Trollkein. Best to just stand there and try to look dangerous until they could make their escape.

"Yes, I think that should do you!" Trollkein said. He gingerly placed the bag of goodies a few feet from the huddled knights, keeping a careful watch on the state of the glowing sword aimed at him. "Now have a good quest, do you hear? And be assured that your names shall live forever in my tales."

He backed away, plainly feeling more at ease the farther he got from Ian's sword. "By the by, Master Farthing, just where did you get that? It has long been the subject of legend among scribblers and warriors alike."

"I . . . I found it!" replied Ian, trying to sound ferocious but ill succeeding. "At a fair!"

Sir Godfrey tugged up the heavy bag, pulled it across his shoulder, and said: "I suggest we depart, my friends. *Bon appetit*, Trollkeins," he said with a gesture toward the filleted Sir Ronald and Sir Stephen. "But be assured, you shall pay for your gustatory sins one day!"

"Found it at a fair?" the troll said bemusedly. "You must be a special creature to use it so effectively. But take my warning, Master Farthing! The Pen That Is Mightier Than the Sword has three edges and can easily bite the wielder!"

On that note, the questing party, still the worse

for drink, stumbled out of the troll home, boarded their horses, and got away as fast as they could.

The last thing that Ian Farthing heard from the house was Mr. Trollkein complaining loudly about the mess.

chapter ten

The Great Nine of the Gaming Magi huddled around the coiled remains of Jason Dunworthy's Wraith Board, attempting to determine what the present gaming conditions were. The task was no mean feat, since, although there were still playing pieces scattered helter-skelter across the board's surfaces, they had been in such a different arrangement before that intense scrutiny was needed. And examination, with the board in its present contorted position, was not an easy proposition!

They had been bickering over the relevance of this piece and the importance of the placement of that group for some time, their voices often punctuated by excited animal sounds, when Crowley Nilrem finally could stand no more and called for silence.

"Gentlemen, please!" he piped in his excellent enunciation. "We are getting absolutely nowhere, and even as we speak events may be taking place that could lead to total ruin!"

In the wake of silence following his outcry, he paused and straightened his waistcoat, more from habit than anything else, since the disarray of his general appearance needed far more than just that gesture. "Now then, I realize that we have never before worked together in this manner, but if we can just take some time to cooperate, I think the fruit of the results will be worth the strain. Now then, Spiffington, old chap. I think we all acknowledge you to be the best of us as far as map and board piece analysis goes. Just what do you make of this mess?"

Spiffington preened a bit, straightening his mustache and then rubbing his flipperlike hands together. He adjusted his tendency to honk in a walrus manner in the first few words and then proceeded to discourse on what he saw upon the Wraith Board.

"Well now, of course, the last thing we were concerned about was the fate of Alandra, who holds a frightening amount of power, and I think that we all should accept culpability for allowing her to become so dangerous!"

"Come, come, fellow," growled Barnum Armbruster. "You know how dull the games were becoming. We had to!"

"Yes, and thus we find ourselves in this devilish situation," neighed Nostril Daymoos, pawing the ground with a hoof. "But please, Spiff. Do carry on!"

"Yes. Alandra. The Key . . . and of course dear Colin Rawlings knows what Roth Kogar and Snirk Morgsteen and even the princess herself do not know. What the Door is!"

A dread silence fell over those assembled. Crowley Nilrem swallowed nervously and found himself fumbling with the dice in his pocket—the Eyes of Ivory. These, like the Die of Dances, were of the Original Set, and carried extraordinary powers.

The Door! Nilrem shuddered at the thought. Spiff was right; they were all responsible. They should never have played with that dreadful artifact, that portal to—

"Pardon me!" gruffed Salvatore Amore, advancing his ponderous belly forward. "But how would Rawlings know?"

The question clearly ruffled Irler Mothwing's feathers. He leaned over and bit the pig's tail with his beak. "Because, ninny, Rawlings created the plans for the Door . . . along with the entirety of the Dark Circle."

"Yes, and from the events that have taken place," Elwood Spiffington continued, "one can only surmise that Rawlings, in whatever combination of spectral and corporeal forms he presently finds himself, is well aware that we have created a Key and that the Key rests with Alandra."

"And so where is Alandra now?" asked Igward T. LePouf, examining the Wraith Board intently from the other side.

Spiffington pointed with a flipper. "Here." The end of his flipper touched a bump portraying a mountain topped with a lump portraying a castle. "I don't know if you all recall the adventure we played with a creature called a dragoon, but this is where it lives—high in its fortress aerie. When I saw that the Alandra piece was nowhere to be seen, I naturally checked the places were it might be hidden, and . . ." He flipped back the top of the mountain. Within huddled the Alandra playing piece—a tiny figure topped with blond hair and arrayed in a gown. Around her neck was a tiny symbolic key. "I found her here. Now, she is perfectly safe for the time being in this place. The dragoon collects odd creatures to be part of its 'family,' and thus apparently it has picked Alandra, wresting her from Morgsteen's Norx, who are quite a distance away and can't scale these walls anyway.''

Crowley Nilrem put on his special pair of eyeglasses and peered into the cavity. Sure enough, right by Alandra's feet was Alabaster's piece. The magus felt relieved.

"Now then," continued the walrus-man, waving his limb toward the torn-apart quadrant of Mormorn, center of Lord Morgsteen's power. "From all signs, the apocalyptic happenings have quite confounded Snirk Morgsteen's armies, to say nothing of Morgsteen himself. He and his powers will not be a force to reckon with for a small time. His magicians will be too busy trying to analyze what has happened and to piece their necromantic systems back together to continue puzzling over the magical nature of the absent Alandra. Still, we would be in error to ignore Morgsteen.''

"And what about the other Dark Lord, Kogar?" asked Nostril Daymoos.

"Apparently still imprisoned in a dungeon of his castle.''

"But I distinctly saw him flying in his ornithopter to intercept Alandra in Mullshire!" Nilrem said, puzzled.

"Yes, well, curiously enough I'm picking up a sense of Kogar's presence elsewhere . . . here with a party of knights who appear from all signs to be from Mullshire, including the Sir Godfrey piece, who, you may recall, we had decided upon as the hero in our rather foolish Adventure of the Key.'' Spiffington cleared his voice as he showed the location of the mentioned group. "Yes, and there are a couple of interesting aspects to this group that I can't quite figure out yet . . . a curious power that I can't recognize."

Nilrem examined the group, and recognized the piece he had seen appear after the debacle of the wrecked playing board. Spiffington was right; the party did emanate a special kind of magic that he could not interpret either.

"Right. Gentlepeople, we have only two options," Spiffington was saying. "Our first is a continuation of our usual methods of operation— namely, magical manipulation of the pieces with our Destiny Dice. Our collected power may be enough to combat the erupted chaos, and then again it may not. Our other option is much less pleasant. As Gaming Magi, should we choose to actually fully enter the plane of the Dark Circle, our Destiny Dice would serve as powerful talismans. We could become powerful magicians there, and thus exert a more direct power. In either case, we will have to deal with Colin Rawlings. And, in either case, from my reading, our best bet is to assist in any manner we can the progress of the aforementioned group of knights. For it is a distinct power of Good and Order that radiates from within them, and the power of Alandra the Key will be used to restore, if not the Old Order, then at least the cause of Law—a cause that, alas, we have diddled with far too much."

"A vote, then?" suggested Barnum Armbruster. "What are the arguments in favor of either alternative?"

As the magi began to discuss minutiae of thaumaturgical strategies and the influence of dice throws as opposed to actual physical intervention, Crowley Nilrem noticed that while they had been embroiled in discussion, Jason Dunworthy had been drawing a pentacle with chalk on the floor, in a manner so as to enclose the group and the Wraith Board. Bemused, Nilrem observed as Dunworthy took a strange-looking pack of tarot cards from a large pocket and, one by one, began to place them perpendicular to the white line.

"I say, Jason," Nilrem said, confused. "Whatever are you doing?"

Dunworthy looked up and met Nilrem's eyes stare for stare. There was something unusual about those dark brown eyes now—something like small cold glitters at the bottom of twin wells. "Just describing a protective diagram, old boy," said Dunworthy. "Can't be too careful with that bounder Rawlings bouncing about!"

Protective diagram? Nilrem wondered as he turned his attention to the important matters being discussed in a thoroughly civilized fashion by the magi, Armbruster leading the debate. Yes, that was one of Dunworthy's specialties, certainly. But he'd never seen anything like what the kneeling magus was doing—and it reminded him of something else he could not place.

As the others droned on, he suddenly remembered. How could he have been so stupid? In all the confusion, he had simply forgotten that Rawlings in his discorporeal form had said that he would contact the collected magi, and appear before them to state demands. But he had not shown up yet in the assembled company . . .

Dunworthy arose and stepped back a few steps, smiling, with an expression that was unusual for the man: a cold, calculating smile. He pulled his hands up, and around each clung a chilly blue nimbus.

. . . or had he?

"Dunworthy?" Nilrem called. "Dunworthy, whatever—"

A stream of light slowly connected the hands and then flowed toward the group gathered around the Wraith Board. Blue light, Nilrem saw. Freeze light.

"Run!" cried Crowley Nilrem to the others as he leaped over the pentacle line and raced toward Jason Dunworthy. But the other magi did not hear him, continuing their loud arguments. Nilrem jumped upon Dunworthy, propelling the man to the floor. But the blue light slid on. Like a stream of horizontal liquid filling up an imaginary bottle whose outlines were described by the chalk pentacle, it collected around the Magi— freezing them instantly, stopping their rumbling voices.

Nilrem rolled around on the floor with Dunworthy, then found himself atop the man. The eyes glistened and glittered, and Nilrem knew that they did not belong to Jason Dunworthy. The realization stunned him so much, he could not strike the blow his fist had risen to deliver.

"Rawlings," he said, staring down in horror. "You've possessed Dunworthy's body!"

"Well, of course, Nilrem! Why do you think you had to roll the Die of Dances? To allow just that! You played right into my hands!"

Furiously, Crowley Nilrem drove his fist down, but Rawlings lifted a hand and caught it by the wrist. "There, there, Nilrem, steady on. Now why don't you be a good fellow and join your companions in their prison, as I planned?"

With a supernatural power, Rawlings hurled Nilrem off him. The magus rolled, sprawling just short of the edge of the pentacle. He looked up and saw that within it, among clotted dazzles and glimmers and traceries of varicolored lights, the Gaming Magi were frozen, quite impotent.

Colin Rawlings had trapped them!

And he, Crowley Nilrem, had been Rawlings's instrument! And the madman wanted to toss him in with the others to languish in the captivity of stasis—perhaps forever!

Nilrem scrabbled to his feet and backed away from the churning body of light, keeping his eye on Colin Rawlings. "I wish we had killed you!"

"But you could not, you know that," Rawlings said as he got to his feet and brushed himself off. "So why even summon the thought?"

"I still don't understand what you want!" Nilrem said. "Why all this madness?"

"Dear boy, why should I tell you everything? Isn't simple vengeance enough?" Rawlings began to move toward Nilrem, rolling up his sleeves as he walked. "Besides, I thought you knew me well enough by now. Of course, our previous encounters were centuries ago, and memories do fade. . . . Now why don't you just be a good little magus and step inside the nice light with the rest of your friends and let me deal with things as I see fit." His eyes widened. "As it should be!"

"Do you think I'm mad as well?" Nilrem said, backing away. "While I live and breathe I'll fight you, Colin Rawlings!"

"Oh, please cut this silly melodrama, man! I only want to change some things around, and then, who knows, I might get bored and want some clever opponents and release you all! Now

hat would be a grand kind of game, don't you
hink? Right now, though, I should like to exile
you all just as I was exiled. To return the favor, so
o speak. But don't fret, magus! It won't hurt.''

Rawlings's hands reached out pointing toward
Nilrem, the blue glow returning, pulsing, growing.

Crowley Nilrem tore his eyes away from the
fascinating tremors of light, and he ran out of the
room for all he was worth.

A flash of light streamed by his ear just as he
turned the corner of the hall and made instinctively for the stairs. He heard the sound of rapid
footsteps pursuing him. He took the stairs three at
a time, racing up to the second floor.

Nilrem leaped into the nearest room to catch
his breath.

Damn! Everything was still falling apart! And
now it was clearly a case of him alone against
Colin Rawlings in this old magic house that was
not his . . . the only magus now standing between
the madman and his plans for this focus point of
the universes!

Crowley Nilrem had definitely seen better days.

He heard Rawlings's stealthy footsteps climbing the stairs, and knew he had to decide what he
was going to do, and fast.

"Oh, come on out, Nilrem. Be a good sport.
You know I've won, and you've been quite a help
all along! So why don't you just come out and go
the extra mile, eh?''

As Nilrem's eyes grew more accustomed to
the dimness in the room, he looked around. There
was no way out other than the door by which he
had entered. He cast about, looking for a possible
weapon, but all he could see was books and stacks
of cardboard boxes. He could hide among the

boxes, but for how long? Rawlings would doubtless find him very soon, and unlike himself, the
recently reincarnated fellow had armed himself
with spells that would make short work of any
fight.

"I shouldn't like to hurt you, Crowley," the
voice called, more distant now. "I dealt with
Dunworthy in this fashion because I needed his
body. I assure you I can restore him, once I fashion a new body for myself. Things will just be a
little different, my good friend! My Games will
need able players like yourself, so why would I
dispose of you permanently?"

The words were tempting, seductive. Why not
just give in, Nilrem thought, join the others? He'd
done his best, and perhaps Rawlings meant what
he said. It would be so easy to give in, and the
magus was weary, so weary not only of this terrible business, but of gaming. It had lately become
more of a chore than a pleasure, and at times
Nilrem had considered retiring. But being a Gaming Magus was like having a tiger by the tail, and
there were always many considerations to think
of before retirement was possible. How easy it
would be, though, to just surrender, give in to
this powerful being. . . .

But no, Nilrem thought, remembering what kind
of person Colin Rawlings had been after the creation of the Dark Circle. The Gaming Magi were
content with their play, happy with the flux and
wane of power, more involved with the Games
than with the thought of personal benefit. This
was why they had all reached these pinnacles in
their playing. The sport was the thing, and there
were compassion and values behind the essential
principles by which they played and for which

they played—the eternal cycles of existence, the give and take between good and evil, the seesaw of law and chaos within and without the universes. They had their roles and they played them nobly.

But Rawlings—

Colin Rawlings was different.

Colin Rawlings had obscure and bizarre ambitions. His cruelties had no gaming integrity, his designs no sense of symmetry. His deeds and machinations had given him a terrible reputation on many worlds, in many universes.

In the world that Crowley Nilrem had come from, Rawlings had been known by many names, but the one that the younger Nilrem had known him by was Lucifer.

But, then, that had been an understatement, for he was so much more. . . .

"Ally, ally in come free!" cried Colin Rawlings, his voice nearing. "I say, Nilrem. We shouldn't behave in this uncivilized manner. I'm just remembering some of the good times we've had together! Why, do you remember when it looked like the goody-goodies were proliferating in the Circle and there were more Bright Lords than you could shake a stick at? Remember how we worked behind the others' backs to rig up the most wonderful set of temptations and subverted at least half of those moral lords into dark and nasty ways? Wasn't that fun? Now, I'm just thinking, you never were totally with the others in my exile procedures, and perhaps we might want to work together again! There are things in existence even beyond the imaginations of the Gaming Magi, Nilrem! Powers and glories and black excitements!

Come out and we'll brew a spot of tea and discuss our partnership!''

Rawlings always had been a persuasive bastard.

But no, that had been centuries ago. Crowley Nilrem had become wiser in time, and he knew he'd rather die first. But, of course, he would rather fight Rawlings, remove the threat of his presence in the multiverse. How, though?

It was then that the magus looked up and noticed the hatch in the ceiling. Doubtless it led to the attic. And in the attic perhaps he might find something of help.

As quietly as he could, the magus began stacking boxes. The result was ramshackle and rickety, but it would have to serve, Nilrem thought, as he scampered up the rudimentary stairway and, balancing carefully, pushed up at the slat of wood fitted in the hatchway.

The wood squeaked against its frame as it moved up and over the edge. Above Nilrem was pure darkness.

The door opened, and Rawlings entered.

"Ah, there you are, Nilrem," he said, folding his arms together. "What do you say to my offer?"

Nilrem hoisted himself up through the hatch. "Let me think about it, Rawlings. Give me a century or so."

"Damn!"

A blaze of energy shot past Nilrem's shoulder, slashing through the darkness and blasting through the roof. Magical fires ate away at wood and shingles, illuminating this section of the huge attic. In the distance, dim shapes draped with tarpaulins hulked like sleeping monsters.

With speed born of desperation, Nilrem pulled

the rest of his body into the attic and rolled away from the hatchway.

"You can't get away, Crowley! I promise you that!" called Rawlings shrilly from below, all tact and manners gone from his voice.

Nilrem looked around. There were places to hide up here, but to what end? Rawlings would certainly find him. Was he just stalling the inevitable?

The sorcerous fire curling about the hole in the roof died with remarkable quickness, leaving a perfectly round hole through which shone stars.

Hardly thinking, Nilrem made for that hole and lifted himself through, up onto the roof. Perhaps there was a way down from here.

A chilly wind caught him immediately, causing him to lose his balance and almost his footing. He moved out of range of any more of Rawlings's firebolts from below, then sank to his knees to recover his bearings.

The roof was steep, bordered by the usual collection of gutters and drainpipes, topped by a varied assortment of chimney pots. Nilrem could see no way down to the ground on this side and determined to check the other. Slowly, he crabbed his way up across the loose shingles, bits and pieces often coming free under his hands or heels. When he reached the top, he hauled himself over by grabbing a ceramic chimney, noting that it cracked under his weight.

Nilrem rested.

A shooting star traversed the starry heavens. A few cirrus clouds stirred overhead, like floating ghosts wandering through space. The wind, stronger up on top of the roof, fluttered the remains of the magus's clothing; he'd have to take that wind into account, lest a sudden gust make him lose his purchase.

The near side of the house, he remembered, was covered with trellised ivy. If he could make his way there, he could climb down.

He glanced back to the hole in the roof. No sign of Rawlings yet. Perhaps the fellow thought he'd hidden in the attic, which was just fine by Nilrem—it would take a long time to search that attic.

Nilrem inched along the top of the roof, using the clusters of chimney pots as resting points. The chill wind bit into his lungs with his heavy breathing. He was not used to so much exercise, what with his sedentary ways, and this whole business put a terrible strain on all his faculties. The air smelled of slate and rot up here; an old smell, above an old house, and it turned the magus's stomach.

Finally, he reached the edge and looked over it.

Sure enough, the side of the house was covered with thick, viny ivy, curling around trellis slats. But most of this side, instead of ending in ground, was cut off. The whole house dangled over raw space. Part of the space-island upon which Jason Dunworthy's mansion had perched had crumbled away, just as Crowley Nilrem's had crumbled.

What was going on?

Still, this afforded an opportunity which he had been seeking by getting down to the ground. With one arm securely leashed about one of the pipes, the magus fished out his pack of tarot cards. All of them had changed into the symbol of the hanged man, but he suspected that this was only a temporary effect on Dunworthy's method of demise.

By the feeble light of the night sky, Nilrem saw that this was true—with one hand he fanned part of the pack out, and saw that they were back to normal.

Hastily, he selected the most stable one—the ace of wands, symbolizing new beginnings—and held it out past the roof but level with it.

"Still using the Tarot Express, eh, Crowley Nilrem?" came Rawlings's voice.

With a gasp, Nilrem turned and saw his foe rising up from the hole in the roof, straight and unaffected by the wind.

How—?

His question was answered immediately. Colin Rawlings stood upon a fiery cloud as though it were a platform. Serenely, he floated through the air up the angle of the roof, toward Crowley Nilrem.

"Oh yes, I know. Godlike. You die and you learn," said Colin Rawlings smugly.

Hastily, Nilrem went back to work, holding the card out and muttering the correct fixing spell. If he could just step out upon the card now—

The blast caught card and deck alight, a brilliant flash of power that scattered them to the winds. They fluttered away, out of reach, into the chasm of sky below.

Nilrem reacted instantly, leaping off the roof and grabbing with one hand a vine and with the other a length of trellis. Hastily, he began to climb down.

If he could reach the ground, perhaps there was still hope, he thought, his heart hammering, his breathing ragged. Perhaps he could dash back into the house, find another deck of cards . . . something, anything. Colin Rawlings had to be stopped, and the chore was left to him alone, of all the responsible Gaming Magi. For if Colin Rawlings obtained the full power that he sought, not even the God of Games knew what would be wrought!

Suddenly, Rawlings's head thrust over the side of the roof.

"Crowley, your persistence amazes me! Why don't you just surrender?"

"You know I can't do that," Nilrem said, still descending desperately. "I can't be responsible for allowing you what you desire! I know something of what you will do—and what you have already done is insufferable!"

Rawlings shook his head. "Spoilsport. I apologize for this desperate measure, Crowley, but face it, your interference has been a thorn in my side. Happy landings!"

Directing a hand downward, Rawlings loosed a firebolt, which exploded just above Nilrem's hands. The whole side of ivy vine and trellis was blown out in a great gout of wood, brick, and masonry.

Crowley Nilrem was hurled back, clutching desperately for purchase but finding only empty air or loose ivy.

He fell toward the fields of stars, Rawlings's chuckle echoing in his ears.

chapter eleven

s far as Ian Farthing was concerned, there had
been just one advantage in being a crippled
and ugly social outcast: His condition had
directly resulted in his ability to read and write,
intellectual skills rare in the medieval climate of his
homeland of Mullshire in the Kingdom of Harleigh.

The only educational system to speak of for a
person of Ian's class was one's family, but his
adoptive parents could not have made him liter-
ate—they themselves could only read and write
as much as was necessary for their cobbling business, and they certainly had neither the money
nor the motivation to gift Ian with a tutor or send
him to a school. A tradesman's son, after all, was
meant to help with the trade and carry on in his
father's footsteps.

However, when he was younger and his duties
with leather and tools were limited, not even in
the apprentice stage yet, Ian Farthing had been
fascinated with the scribbles and scrawls of writing, with the whole idea of meaning being as-
cribed to a series of characters, and then meanings
piled upon meanings until a complex message or
story was related.

So, when the opportunity arose for him to shed his illiterate state, he grasped it with both his gnarled hands.

He had gotten that opportunity in this fashion:

One Sabbath, as a child of eleven, he had been wandering the grounds of the town's most imposing architectural structure aside from Baron Richard's castle: its cathedral. Mullshire Cathedral was the usual monolithic collection of spires and towers and flying buttresses rearing up toward Heaven like one of God's footstools. Ian had marveled in its incense-filled and stained-glass interiors reverberating with chants more than once, getting a strange excitement out of the numinous qualities haunting the vaulted chambers and passageways. But that was not why he had come there that day. He had come to walk in the gardens and grounds surrounding the structure.

This was not a general practice among Mull folk, so Ian found the quiet and solitude among the neatly kept trees, clipped bushes, and patterned flowers refreshing after the drudgery of helping his father. And he certainly preferred it to the cruel company of his peers in the streets.

On that fateful day, he had stumbled upon a monk sitting on the ground trying to repair a broken sandal. Through sign language, Ian had offered to help the monk. The fellow, one Brother Theodore, had taken him back to his spartan quarters and provided him with the sort of needle and thread he'd requested. Ian had refused payment—but had requested to look through some of the laboriously hand-lettered and illuminated volumes on the monk's shelves.

Ian was able to pick out this or that Latin word, but was otherwise ignorant of what the book said.

But the pictures and fancy lettering were beautiful, and Ian recognized scenes from the Bible and the lives of the saints that he remembered from the mystery and miracle and morality plays he'd seen parade in the streets, medieval catechism. Ian's fascination was not lost on Brother Theodore. A good and godly man, the monk had been impressed with Ian's skill with shoes, and he recognized the lad's goodness and gentleness of nature beneath the ugly shell. He had explained the meaning of some of the words and had marveled how Ian's eyes had shone with eagerness. A deal was struck: Ian could borrow the book. Every Sunday afternoon, he could return to the abbey and repair the shoes of the brothers. In return, Brother Theodore would teach him to read and write.

Ian had been thrilled.

Sunday afternoons came to be his favorite time of the week, and Brother Theodore's task proved to be an easy one, for the lad stayed up late at night with candles, puzzling out words and grammar, copying letters in his crabbed hand, and the time was soon spent more in the answering of questions than in actual instruction. Soon Ian was borrowing the valuable books at a faster pace, and before long he was able to compose letters and essays and such.

However, as the years passed, he had to take on more and more duties at home, and had to reduce both his work with books and his visits to the abbey. Which was just as well, really, he knew, because if his da had caught him giving away his business for book learning instead of shillings, he would have been in bad shape indeed.

His talents gave him the secret and delightful

opportunity of a private life away from the social cesspool of those who despised the way he walked, talked, and looked. Those clods could barely make their signs, and he could read and write. Still, whenever he displayed his abilities among his peers, he was roundly ridiculed and drubbed, and the effect was to alienate Ian even further.

Brother Theodore had lived to the ripe old age of forty-two, and the other monks had not been so kind about the lending of their precious books, and so Ian had to write his own little stories in Latin to entertain himself, settling for rereading the volume that the dear monk had left him: a Bible.

Now as Ian rode across the landscape of the Dark Circle, observing and sometimes interacting with the odd denizens and dangers, he wished he had paper and time enough to write down his thoughts and feelings and to detail the steps of this strange odyssey.

He certainly had a pen, though he was afraid to use it in fear of accidentally shredding anything he wrote upon.

Yes, he thought as he rode through forest and dale, field and vale, how could Latin words on parchment describe what had happened in this past day alone, even if he had enough energy to scribble them?

After fleeing the Trollkein "cottage," leaving behind two of their companions with pie shells and troll stomachs their coffins and graves, they had struck out once more. In very short time, they had overtaken Alison Gross, huffing and puffing along, terror-stricken.

The single fortunate aspect of their violent encounter with the trolls had been that now they had enough horses for everyone, and could travel at a better speed. Once they had settled down after their unfortunate adventure with the trolls, and sobered up as well, Sir Godfrey proclaimed that they had traveled far enough to be out of danger. They halted for a brief meeting, bringing out Kogar's robot head for consultation.

Alas, they had not been able to raise the fellow.

"What's to be done then?" Sir Oscar said, despondently crouching down in the glade for some rest after making sure that no further trolls lurked in the bushes. "Already three of our number are dead, and we've been gone only a few days!"

"You all knew the risks," Sir Godfrey Pinkham said, pawing through the contents of the burlap bag. "Be assured that brothers Mallory, Komquatte, and Jentile are in heaven now, already receiving the eternal reward for their valor."

"Not a bloody lot of good that does us down here!" Sir William grumbled, staring morosely into the woods through reddened eyes.

"Aye, but we're all to be blamed," Sir Mortimer said, flat on his back, eyes closed. "Our stupidity, our gullibility, our greed—but we must take it as a lesson for later on. We must remember that not just the contents of our pockets or our stomachs are at stake, but the welfare of us all."

Sir Godfrey tied the sack back up and fitted it to the spare horse. "How true, how true," he said, going back to the ground where Kogar's head sat mute. He tapped it. "Come on, then, Dark Lord. What's next?"

The head did not respond.

"Aren't you going to ask me?" Alison Gross demanded.

Ian was startled. When they had stopped, the

hag had crumpled into a heap, seemingly unconscious from the ordeal.

"Yes," Hillary said. "Perhaps we should listen to Alison more. We wouldn't have gone into that troll's awful cottage if we'd heeded her trepidations! Certainly would be a sight better than anything we can learn from that head. Gives me the creeps anyway."

"Yes, of course. Do go on, er—madam."

"We're headed in the right direction, sure enough, if I've got my headings right," she said, shakily regaining her feet. "Now, I've been thinkin'. From what I could see from when I got hauled ass over ankles across the territory, if we stick to the land, then it would take us weeks and weeks to get around to Princerik's Keep. That's 'cause the land got split up, you know."

"So you suggest some sort of sea trip?" Sir Oscar said, sitting up and taking interest.

"No, no! I want to go back same way I got here!" She wiggled a finger upward. "The air!"

"Oh yes, I believe you mentioned that possibility sometime back," said Sir Godfrey. "But pray tell, how are we going to accomplish that task? Sprout wings and fly? With what we've seen so far in this accursed land, I should not be surprised!"

"No, no. If my reckonin' be right, there's a town about a day's journey by horseback. Called Knavesville. I've been around, believe me, and normally I'd avoid the place. For some reason it tends to collect the evil rogues and thieves of the Circle. Maybe because it's a brewery town and they can get cheap drinks at taverns. Anyway, I know this guy, has a stable of wyverns for hire."

"Wyverns?" Sir William said.

"The Model T of dragons," Alison explained.

"But good passenger carriers. Old and tame, couple thousand years old, few holes in the wings, but steady. So now we've got some coin from that troll, we can hire out a couple of the beasts and be at Princerik's Keep in two shakes of a belphagor's tail!"

"And you will be able to guide us to this Keep—through the air? You can control these wyverns?"

"Hey—does the pope shit on the bears? But of course—I used to go with this guy. He's got orc in his blood, and was he ever handsome in his century!"

Since they could not raise Kogar for corroboration, the party decided that as Alison Gross's plan sounded not only likely but speedy, they would head toward Knavesville.

Ian Farthing was not precisely keen on the idea of flying Dragon Express, but along with Hillary he agreed that time was of the essence. Hillary had, of late, started to speak with more and more concern of home.

"After all," she pointed out, "we did leave Mullshire in rather a mess. I do hope my parents are all right." This the next morning, as they rode abreast upon an increasingly well-defined road toward Knavesville.

"That's one of the reasons we're here," Ian reminded her. "We can't help them much back there without succeeding in this wretched quest, I'm afraid."

"Yes, yes, you're quite right," said Hillary. "Thank you, Ian. I must say, I didn't expect that from you. You have changed, haven't you? More than just in your appearance." She was looking at him with a funny expression.

Ian turned away and said nothing, for he knew

she was right. And the truth was that the changes happening inside him were scarier to him than those that had happened to Mullshire.

I'm a selfish bastard, then, aren't I? Ian thought to himself. Only concerned about myself. So what if I'm scared? Who the hell wouldn't be, in this kind of situation, traveling through a land where just about anything can happen, and probably will?

After a while, he said, "Hillary, maybe you're right. But what good will it do? What good will it do you or me or Mullshire that I'm changing?"

She brightened. "We'll just have to wait and see, won't we? And that's something definitely more worth questing for than a silly beautiful princess!"

"One thing is for sure . . . you haven't changed!" Ian laughed.

"If I did, you'd be lost without me!" Hillary stuck her tongue out and galloped ahead of him, laughing girlishly.

The day was uneventful and actually quite lovely, and Ian felt a strange kind of peace inside of him as they rode quietly through it, contemplating what he would write down now if he could. Probably something about how he felt he was changing—though how would you write that in Latin?

Most times, he had to admit to himself, admiring the way the sun gilded a bank of clouds, then poured down gently upon a field of poppies, most times, words just wouldn't do.

As the hag had predicted, they reached Knavesville late in the afternoon. Which was just as well, since they could have gone no farther in that direction.

For the land abruptly—stopped.

The change was quite clean, as though a sharp knife had sliced through the ground. Land gave way perpendicularly to sky. Beyond, amid the darkening clouds, rose the next strip of the land, formerly attached to this one. But it was faint in the distance, and between there was a chasm miles long.

"That," Alison said blithely, pointing, "is what we're going to have to get our rear ends over."

Sir Oscar was quick to note that the town of Knavesville had been cleanly cut in half in the cataclysm. "Let's just hope that your friend's tavern didn't end up on the other side."

"No worry," said Alison. "Both tavern and stables are well to this side of the town, as my expert memory recalls."

"And if not?" Sir Godfrey spat nastily.

"With the right money, one can buy many kinds of services in a town like Knavesville. A warning, though. Dusk approaches. As we enter the city, keep close. Brigands, cutpurses, highwaymen, robbers, murderers—this place has them all, and many have magic to boot!"

"What stops them from killing each other off?" Ian asked, inwardly cringing at the thought of a whole clutch of nasties taking a moment from each other's throats to have a swipe at the new gimpy fool in town.

"Honor among thieves?" suggested Sir Oscar.

"Pah!" said Alison. "A myth if I ever heard one! No, when they're in Knavesville they're either too drunk to bother, or they're resting from some chicanery elsewhere and haven't the energy. Still, it's a damned violent town, so beware!''

"Do you think it's a good idea then to enter wearing the clothing of good and noble people when this is what thieves will naturally despise?'' asked Hillary.

"A good point," said Ian. "Perhaps you knights should at least take off your coats of arms and attempt to look more disreputable!''

"Never!" Sir Godfrey cried. "Valor shall be our shield against evil.''

"You're crazy, mate!" Sir Mortimer promptly ripped off the symbols of his family from his uniform and stuffed them into his satchel. "It's easier to sew these back on than to stuff one's innards back in!''

Sir Oscar and Sir William followed suit, jumping to the ground and dirtying their faces and mussing their hair. "If anyone asks, we stole this mail and these weapons!" said Sir William. "And we suggest, Godfrey, that you shake a spear and recall that discretion is the better part of valor!''

Sir Godfrey was reluctantly forced to comply with the others' wishes. Ian and Hillary decided that their serf's outfits were suitable, but Alison insisted on dirtying her face to prevent rapists from noting and lusting after her beauty.

Once the party deemed themselves scruffy enough (and they had to aid Sir Godfrey Pinkham, a task which Ian took much pleasure in, supplying the dirt as the others held the knight down), they proceeded to enter the town known as Knavesville.

In architecture, Ian noted, the place was not dissimilar to Mull, though its storied buildings and huts and such were not packed so closely together. Instead of the predominant features being cathedral and castle, however, the large buildings there were the several breweries, from which the rich scent of ale emanated, permeating the air.

There the similarity to Mull ended, however, for the populace was by no means the average crop of medieval workers, tradesmen, knights, and such.

Instead, the place was like a carnival of fantasy, its denizens wearing all manner of dissimilar clothing from different lands and different worlds.

Thanks to their tattered clothing, they were largely ignored when they traipsed into town, just as torches were being lit against the coming dusk. Under Alison Gross's lead, they rode their horses slowly down the straight road past halls and stalls, alleys and stoops occupied by elves and dwarves, orcs and men and other creatures that Ian found it difficult to identify.

By the time they had reached the tavern, it was dark.

"I hope they serve food," said Hillary, voicing Ian's own thoughts. "I'm hungry."

Ian could smell roast meat. "I don't think there will be a problem with that!" His stomach rumbled hungrily in sympathy with Hillary's sentiments.

Over the heavily hinged front door of the tavern hung a wooden sign proclaiming: FISHER'S BAR AND GRAIL. Voices, human and otherwise, emanated, some in song. They parked their horses in a misty alley and paid coin to a boy to watch them. Then Alison Gross led them through a side door into the tavern.

A smoky blast of warmth met Ian as he stepped through the door, following the others. He smelled charred meat, baking bread, wine, and beer—a delicious mixture, reminiscent of the times that Da had taken him to the Ox and Ax back in Mull. The low-slung ceiling hung supported by brown timbers over a motley collection of drinkers and eaters and roisterers. Mead and ale spilled on sawdust as tavern wenches carried ceramic pitchers of the stuff to thirsty ruffians clustered together in groups around oaken tables.

No notice was taken of the new arrivals.

"Come on, then," Alison insisted as the group slowed to stare at the scene. "Barkamus Thur will be back in his usual place at this time. Hurry and we can eat some grub with him."

They shuffled back and past a mammoth hearth full of spitted chickens and pigs and other less recognizable animals. Ian coughed, his eyes tearing at the smoke, but fortunately, Alison led them deeper into the candle-and-torch-lit interior.

At first, Ian had taken heart in the familiarity of this place—its smells, its warmth, the clink of flagon and cup, the chomp of meat pies; all reminded him of home. But as his eyes grew accustomed to the dimness, with its pockets of shadow and brightness, he realized with a shiver of fright that the tavern was—different.

Instead of the usual medieval garb of capuchon and cloak, breeches and boots, its denizens wore a bewildering array of garb. Lace grew at some of the drinkers' throats and sleeves. Tricornered hats bobbed here and there. Everything was much more colorful than he was used to. Too, familiarity was mocked by the number of nonmen in the place, the squat and swarthy dwarves, the skinny and elegantly attired elves with their pointy ears, their rapier noses. The din was punctuated with the belches of orcs, the farts of gnomes (both legendary in the tales Ian had heard and where he immediately wished they would stay), and soon Ian could tell that the mingle of voices was a far cry from Harleigh English, being instead a disconcerting conglomerate of accents and dialects and languages of amazing variety. Many of these men and creatures looked too finely dressed to be the sort of thieves Ian was familiar with—but then the tales he knew hinted at wealthy robbers, and certainly this place confirmed that notion!

Hillary kept close, eyes wide and hand tucked under one of Ian's arms, as they made their way to the very back, where the darkness was segmented into a series of booths.

Suddenly, Alison halted them. "Stay here a moment. Barkamus doesn't like large groups jumping down on him. Makes him nervous."

"Understandable," said Sir Mortimer, eyeing a foamy tankard thirstily, but keeping a hand on the pommel of his sword.

Ian watched as Alison forged ahead into the gloom. Just before the wall, she stopped, leaned over, and spoke. A small yelp of alarm was buried by the crush of other voices.

"Ian!" Hillary tugged hard at Ian's sleeve. "Is she all right?"

"I don't think that was our Alison's voice," said Sir Mortimer.

"Aye," Sir William agreed. "Should a face like that come peerin' down at me, I should be startled as well."

A few moments of animated chatter later, Alison Gross bustled back, a smile on her face. "As I thought! Barky's there every dusk, havin' his dinner. He's an ample booth, and he's invited us all to join him—provided we pick up the tab."

Sir Godfrey jingled his saddlebags, filled with the stuff obtained from Trollkein. "That's one problem we don't have, just as long as they accept gold or silver or gems here." His voice was ironic.

"Sshhhh!" said Alison Gross. "Do I have to remind you about the clientele?"

She hustled them over to the booth table and motioned to them to sit down on either side.

The sole occupant was huddled in the far corner beside a plate mounded high with stew, a stack of bread, and a pitcher and cup. A candle guttered, flickering its light over features that seemed carved from rough clay. He was a short and hairy man, this Barkamus Thur, thought Ian. And with his dark and deep-set eyes, barely glimmering in the slight light, and his low slouched leather hat, he didn't look particularly friendly or trustworthy. This would be their first test of Alison Gross, and Ian prayed she would pass it, for all their sakes.

"Ah ha! Welcome, hungry people!" the orcish man pronounced in a surprisingly musical voice. His accent was touched with a Celtic lilt, and instantly it calmed Ian's suspicions somewhat. "Please do sit down and I'll call out for Margery to wait upon your needs." He lifted his hat up and sat forward, so that Ian could see that his eyes shone a startlingly emerald sheen. "I trust you've got the oddments of financial security Alison spoke of!"

Sir Godfrey pulled out a few coins and slapped them haughtily upon the table. "And there's more, as well."

Barkamus Thur's eyes twinkled as he took a drink from his cup. "Aye, and Alison's not steered me wrong, no, never. You've come at a good time, my dear. Times are confusing, and a healthy larder is always needed."

Introductions were quickly made. The waitress, the prerequisitely buxom sort, took their order for a huge supply of roast fowl and whatever else the establishment kept in the way of food, to be washed down by healthy quantities of ale. When his cup came, however, Ian only sipped his drink, remembering painfully the experience the other day at the Trollkeins. But the memory did not seem to dampen the others' thirsts at all.

The knights, happy to be in a place at least partially familiar after their long journey, made conversation with Barkamus Thur, who proved to be a manling with the gift of gab. He spoke of the dangerous but exhilarating life in a town of criminals as though it were a constant challenge, a game of extraordinary dimensions.

"We understand, Master Thur," Sir Godfrey said, delicately placing gnawed chicken leg down upon his plate and wiping his hands upon Ian's clothes, "that you keep a stable of winged creatures suitable for transportation."

"And indeed I do!" said the manling. "Alison mentioned you had such needs, and since you seem to have ample funds, my precious wyverns are at your disposal. But let us finish our repast first, and then I shall take you to them."

The knights, still greedily consuming the chow, could only concur.

"But in the meantime, my new associates," said the wyvernkeeper, "you must excuse me. The backhouse beckons."

The squat creature gestured for those who sat on his side of the booth to allow him to pass, and then scooted off and wobbled away.

"For the first time, Alison Gross," Sir Godfrey said expansively, lofting his cup in salute, "I am actually happy you joined our company. You have done us well! Let us toast our dear friend, for I sense our journey is coming to a successful finish!"

Alison Gross giggled and drank, and even Hillary, not usually one for indulging in brew ("Such a wretched taste!" she would complain to Ian), lifted her cup and sipped some happily.

But Ian did not.

Curiously, he felt very ill at ease, but did not know why. The bumps at the back of his neck seemed to be acting up—they throbbed a bit, felt slightly hot. He supposed that perhaps he was anxious in the presence of all these supposedly villainous sorts, and put the matter at the back of his mind, filling up on the meal, realizing it might be his last substantial one for a while. Still, since he was on the end of the booth, he would sneak occasional peeks into the smoky room beyond, just to reassure himself.

Curiously, as he looked at the room, it would sometimes blur and change into subtly different scenes, with different creatures, slurring into different musics. It was as though this were the archtypal dim bar, central to all drinking establishments on all the worlds in all the universes— and from time to time one could peer past this one into the others.

Ian shivered and turned his attention back to the tasty and reasonably wholesome food.

In time, Barkamus Thur returned, looking very pleased with himself. "Yes, I believe that in a very short time we can consider making our way to my stables."

"Just a moment," said Sir Oscar. "Would it be possible to have a night's rest first before we flap off into the unknown?"

"Oh, that can certainly be arranged," said Barkamus. "But, alas, the only room I can arrange is in the stables."

"A pity," said Sir Godfrey. "Still, straw is better than the ground we have gotten used to, and any other sleeping place might well prove to be hazardous in such a town as this."

"You are a wise man," said Barkamus Thur. "And I shall charge you very little extra for the space. Now then, Alison, dear, we have not seen you for a very long time here in Knavesville."

" 'Tis true, 'tis true," said Alison, "for I was carried off by a wonderful dragoon and kept in his Keep for several years. However, as you know, times have been—disruptive. I journey now to rejoin my love, with the help of my retinue!"

Sir Godfrey's eyebrows arose at this, but for once he was wise enough to keep his mouth shut.

"Oh, they protect your fair self from harm as you travel through this dangerous countryside! How noble of them—and, of course, since they are knights, as you say, that is their purpose in life!"

Sir Oscar choked on his beer, but said nothing.

"Now then, perhaps you would like to hear something of my pretties, my witty wyverns, and how they can be used to bear passengers!"

The others readily agreed that this would be an excellent notion. Hillary's eyes in particular shone with curiosity.

"You must understand that I have other busi-

ness concerns," said Barkamus. "You might call
me an entrepreneur extraordinaire!"

"Yes," agreed Alison. "If it has money attached
to it, my pal Barkamus is interested!"

"Well now, one day years back I was sitting in
this selfsame tavern, at the bar, when in walks
this character in a checkered suit asking if anyone would be interested in buying a Brooklyn
Bridge. Now, I always talk to salesmen, but I
made sure the fellow knew I wasn't interested in
any kind of bridge. Did he have anything else he
was interested in selling?

" 'Well,' says he. 'I've got these peculiar old
flying dragons I picked up a while back that I've
not been able to unload but I don't think you'd be
interested.' "

The bumps in Ian's neck twitched.

Abruptly, an unexplainable spurt of fear moved
through him. He jerked around and looked back
out into the tavern.

There, standing by the bar, were two unmistakable figures, their dead eyes surveying the room
stolidly, their thick bodies protruding with muscles and knobs beneath chain mail.

He had last seen this pair on Jat's Pass, through
which they had pursued Alandra via horseback.

Norx!

chapter twelve

"So off on her very own adventures struts Princess Alandra, her scruffy gold-and-silver cat in tow!

"Resolute upon finding the hag's mirror, she journeys into the corridor of Princerik's Keep, a bold and beautiful Amazon who usually gets what she wants!

"Brave Alandra!

"Noble princess—"

"Rotten mistress!" grouched the cat in her arms.

Alandra stopped in midstride and looked down at Alabaster.

"You have complaints, Mr. Cat?"

"Yes, indeed I do! Please, explain to me again why I am being forced to accompany you on this foolish mission," the cat demanded.

"I thought you wanted to go," Alandra said, quite vexed.

Alabaster stared off down the dark and mysterious hallway. "I think my supply of curiosity has run quite dry."

Alandra shook her head wearily. "Oh posh!"

"Woe, oh woe!" The hairs on the cat had begun to rise. "I feel a foreshadow tredding on my grave!"

Alandra gazed down at the passageway. True, the gloom there was quite palpable, a gluey dark that seemed to ooze around the torches in their sconces. So far she had only been in rooms with windows, comfy fires, and candles. Here the cold seemed to reach out with damp fingers and claw at her toes. Odd sounds clicked and echoed up from the drafty stairwell at the end of the hall.

But she was a princess of charm, a charmed bit of royal fluff indeed, and no harm could come to her!

Besides:

"Alabaster. Do you really think that if there were any kind of true danger down there, Princerik would allow me to go down in search of the hag's quarters?"

"I suppose not!" Still, the feline shivered and nuzzled close to her silken blouse.

"Who knows?" she whispered into his ear, his whiskers tickling her cheek. "We may even find a way out!"

"That's one of the things that frightens me," the cat replied.

The mouth at the stairwell breathed up hints of ice and mold and rot. Alandra let the cat down gently and picked up one of the torches from its holder, and together they descended the gray stone steps, coiling down into sibilant near-silence.

"I wonder just what that mirror is, Alabaster," she said in a low voice. Her voice rang in the hollowness like felt-tipped chimes. "I saw my face in that hag's mirror, you know. That must mean something. And my face—it was different! Older, perhaps even more majestic and noble. And Alley, it looked sad! So very sad! I must know why!"

Alabaster padded behind her warily, close enough to keep in the pool of torchlight, but far enough away not to trip her. "Mistress, yours has not been a terribly happy life lately! Father killed! Married to a despicable Dark Lord! Chased by fiendish foul-smelling Norx! Carried away by a lizard-winged goon! These are not happy times!"

"I am perhaps, however, the daughter of an angel, Alabaster," said Alandra soberly. "I am the daughter of a great king, and heiress to destiny." She stopped and nodded resolutely to herself. "Besides, whoever heard of a ravishingly beautiful, breathtaking fairy-tale kind of princess who didn't have a kink or two in her life?" She resolutely continued her march. "But I am optimistic, Alabaster! I believe in myself, and I believe in happy endings."

"And I believe I'd like to wake up and find this all a dream," the cat whined.

"Perhaps a nice sprightly song will cheer you up, Alley. After all, the acoustics are splendid."

"Spare me!"

"But I'm a very excellent singer. Would you like to hear 'Somewhere My Prince Is Waiting,' or 'Whistle While You Work'?"

" 'Night on Bald Mountain' would be more appropriate in this place."

"Look, down there! Another floor. Perhaps we can find someone who knows how to get to Alison Gross's quarters."

They stepped into another corridor. A breeze whipped the flame of the torch about, tousling Alandra's hair and the ends of her dress. The draft seemed to sing through the hall, as though it were the interior of a flute, and the doors that filed down the passageway the stops. Lights seeped

from the doorways like intimations of day. The
princess and the cat wandered down the dreamy
way, in search of this flute's tune.

"Let's check here," Alandra said, quietly, in
deference to the pervasive sense of mystery in the
air. She stopped by the first door and pushed it
back.

The light that flooded through caused them to
squint after the dimness of the corridor. Inside
the room a hundred candles burned among the
smell of incense. Some kind of priest, robed in
black, knelt at an altar amid a bewildering array
of religious symbols.

Alandra cleared her throat. When the man did
not respond to that sound, she said, "Excuse me,
sir!"

The priest jumped up, his bald pate shining in
the candlelight. Startled eyes glanced around the
room, settling quickly upon Alandra. Then a wide
grin split the top of a long beard. "Ah! A new
member of the order!"

Alandra identified herself. "And who are you?"

"Father Brother Reverend Rabbi, at your service!" replied the man courteously with a gentle
bow. "I keep the chapel here for our Lord Princerik.
It specifically sought out my services, since it
doesn't allow the members of its ensemble liberty
to depart to attend the services of their choice. So
it is my privilege and my duty to perform those
services for them!" The robed man pointed to a
collection of books on a teetering shelf from
which dangled a fat spider. "I'm versed in all
manner of spiritual disciplines, madam."

"But how is that possible? Don't they all conflict? Besides, I know for a fact that my faith is
the only true Way."

"Yes, of course!" assured the priest patronizingly. "But haven't you noticed that everyone feels that way? I mean, it comes built into the dogma. But if you just removed that little cornerstone, all religions would fall together and be like parts of one magnificent structure."

Alandra shook her blond tresses adamantly. "No. There's just one God, and he's my God!"

"I assure you that if you look very closely, you'll see they're all largely balderdash and hot air collected about magical reality constructs. But then, I don't mean to get too theological for you."

"My God is whoever feeds me," said Alabaster, yawning, clearly seeing no danger in this gentleman. "Feeds me and pets me and cleans my cat box."

"Exactly. But don't you think that we all create our own God? It depends largely on what's hot on the godly top forty of the universe!" He pointed to his array of crosses, mandalas, circles, squares, and other bewildering geometric designs. "Me, I'm in the Religious Relic of the Month Club, so I get all kinds of stuff from worlds you would not believe. I'm only actually displaying those items appropriate to my clients here in Princerik's Keep. Believe me, I've plenty of idol time around here!" He put his hands on his round abdomen and rumbled with laughter.

"But what about you, Father?" Alandra asked, not knowing what else to call him. "Who is your God?"

The priest smote the air with a finger. "Ah ha! I'm glad you asked me that, my dear. Personally, I belong to the obscure Cult of Mr. Nobody—the powerful and pervasive force in the Universe who is everywhere at once, yet nowhere at all. This is

why I can, with total integrity, exercise the rites
in all these delightful religions. I believe in none,
yet I know all are true. Behold, the sign of my
order!"

He lifted a chain from the depths of his robes.
It showed a waterfowl in a sailor suit, holding
wings with another waterfowl in a dress. "A pair
o' ducks! Our twin patron saints, Donald and
Daisy!" He smiled in a congenial manner and
placed the chain back. "Now then. Has Lord
Princerik sent you down for a ceremony, a prayer?
Do you want a turn of a prayer wheel, a kiss of
ghost dust? My, you're a pretty thing! I can see
why Princerik collected you!"

"Actually," Alandra said, "I was hoping for
some help in locating a certain room. This establishment once was occupied by a hag by the name
of Alison Gross."

"Alison Gross ... oh my yes, a Hindustani
Kalibaptist with gypsy tendencies. Om, Om on
the range and all that. I had to special-order water
from the Ganges and the Mississippi as well for
her immersion rituals. Mind you, Princerik has
all the funds, but it's quite difficult special-ordering.
And with all the hullabaloo in the Cosmos Mail
lately, it's virtually impossible!"

"Well, you won't have to worry about that anymore. She's vacated the premises. I had hoped to
find her room and perhaps think about decorat-
ing those accommodations for myself and my cat
Alabaster."

"Gone? Well, let me see if I can recall ..." He
scratched his beard. "Yes, I believe I was once
summoned to attempt a faith healing on a case of
constipation for that very large and very ugly
lady. You head down the corridor to your left,

catch the flight of stairs two floors down, turn right by the mummy, turn left by the torture dungeon, and it's the suite at the end of the corridor."

Alabaster shivered. "Can I stay here and worship a tin of tuna fish?"

"What?" said the priest. "I should think that a feline should be very comfortable in catacombs!" The priest boomed with laughter.

"I fear that my poor cat shuns grooming," said Alandra, picking her pet up. "But I thank you, sir, for your directions, even if I find your faiths heretical, to say the least."

"Heretical today, gonetical tomorrow!" the priest said.

"What?" Alandra said.

"In such a mausoleumlike place, can I be aught but cryptic?" The priest smiled serenely.

"I think, mistress, it would be a grave mistake to go farther," Alabaster said as a wind howled in distant corridors like a lost soul.

"I am determined!" Alandra said. "And Alabaster, you'll find out soon enough that I generally get what I want."

"Princess Alandra, do be careful with that mirror," said the priest as he turned to light more candles. "Remember my motto: Magic can be tragic!"

Startled, Alandra turned back to ask the priest how he knew the truth of what she wanted in the hag's room.

But the robed man had disappeared into thin air.

"Stricken down by God himself for blasphemy," Alandra declared self-righteously, but with little conviction.

"You see, mistress? You don't want that stupid mirror! Let's go back!"

But Alandra would have none of it. "I want that mirror!" And she placed a firmer hold on the reluctant kitty and hurried down the hallway toward the next stairwell, passing rooms from which mutters and murmurs emerged—passing them quickly.

A growl, a squeak. A whimper: Alabaster's whimper.

But the princess's swift feet made short work of the hall, and she essayed the stairwell with ease. Finally she emerged into the corridor which the priest claimed to be the one holding Alison's chambers.

The passageway was no brighter than the others. As they passed the half-closed doors, they received brief glimpses of strangely decorated rooms—rooms reverberant with soft sounds, snarls, sea-hisses.

Finally, they arrived at their destination. Alandra consulted her runes, who assured her that they had reached the right place.

The door—thick wood, iron hinges—was closed.

"Don't you think you'd better knock?" Alabaster suggested.

"What for?" The princess set the cat down; it wasn't likely he'd try to make it back upstairs alone. "The hag is gone!" The hinges squeaked as she swung back the door. Her torch revealed spacious quarters indeed, full of pillows and carpets, hung with tapestries and draperies predominantly mauve and purple. Alandra quickly found several oil lamps and lit them, dashing light throughout the room, revealing another door into darkness.

"Now. Where is that confounded mirror? I have

he distinct feeling that it will be very useful to
ne, Alabaster—and the runes confirm my feel-
ngs!"

"Mirror, mirror!" Alabaster called out, stalking
orward, having decided to get this over with as
quickly as possible. "Would you care to lend
your reflections on that last statement?"

A terrible barking burst from the adjacent room.
A piece of darkness separated from the mass, and
a snarling collection of teeth and fangs gnashed
and gashed its way across the rug.

"A dog!" Alabaster cried. With one bound, the
cat was back in her arms, burying his claws in
her gown, all twitches, whiskers, and outstanding
fur. "It's a dog, mistress! Oh, save me! Please save
your loving servant!"

"Oh bother," said Alandra. "You're overreacting,
cat! I mean, it could have been an awful monster
or something."

The dog stopped dead in its tracks, its growl
bitten off abruptly. It was only an average-sized
pooch, a black mongrel with floppy ears, large
eyes, a large set of choppers, and an ample amount
of canine claws. Its single distinguishing features
were the three large bushy tails sprouting from its
posterior.

"Wait a goddam minute, lady. I am a monster!"

"Well, you certainly don't look like a monster
to me!" Alandra reiterated assertively. "And if
you are, you're the silliest-looking monster I've
ever seen!"

The beast shook with vexation. "Lady! What do
you think these things are? Floor mops?" It wagged
them with great frenzy.

"Three tails? So what? A freak is not necessarily a monster. Now if you could be so kind, would

you please tell me where I could find Alison Gross's hand mirror. The one ringed with pentagrams, I believe."

"One minute! First things first!" The dog growled huffily. "I will have you know that my brother's name is Cerberus. Ring any bells, lady?"

"Cerberus!" Alabaster squeaked. "He's the three-headed dog that guards the entrance to Hades!"

"Your shabby tabby's dead right. And my name is Herbivorous!"

"Well, Herb, I am impressed! Now how about cueing us in on the whereabouts of that mirror I mentioned?"

The three-tailed dog snarled with fury. "You think I'm here for my health, lady? I'm Alison Gross's guard monster! I'm here to prevent the entrance of people like you. So, unless you'd like to be thoroughly mauled"—the dog clacked its teeth—"I suggest you depart, posthaste."

"You labor under a misapprehension, oh dog. The person you speak of has recently been banished from these premises. So perhaps you'd better keep in mind the source of future dinners!"

"I confess I am a bit peckish. Ah! That cat will do for a start."

Alandra looked down at Alabaster's furry head.

Now here, she thought, is a survivor! If this cat can deal with magic, a magus, a terrible fall, Norx, and God knows what other kinds of danger, then surely it can deal with a measly three-tailed dog!

"Oh well, Herbivorous, if you can catch him you can have him."

"What?" Alabaster screeched.

But before the cat could bury clinging claws into Alandra's gown, the princess had hurled him clear to the far side of the room and onto a divan.

Dust puffed. Doilies scattered. Cat claws tore material as Alabaster scrambled to the top of the seat, glaring back at Alandra.

Following its doggish instincts, Herbivorous, brother to Cerberus, swiveled about, its hackles high, and commenced to enter into a frenzy of barking.

Alandra took the opportunity to grab a lamp and steal into the next room. There she found a very girlish spread of canopied bed, fluffy lace pillows, dainty chairs, curlicued wardrobe, and elaborately carved dresser. All about the room were scattered dolls—dolls of every type and description. Plastic dolls and cloth dolls, stuffed dolls and ceramic dolls. Alandra loved dolls, and she envied the hag her collection. But a sudden screeching and caterwauling from the next room rapidly brought her back to the present.

Where would Alison keep a mirror?

But of course! On the dresser!

She carried the lamp to the other side of the room and sifted through the mounds of junk. There were stacked boxes of jewelry and bottles of perfume and powder puffs, the usual female detritus, flanked by a Barbie doll and a Ken doll. Below a flowered box of Kleenex was the mirror, face down.

Alandra reached for it.

"Hold!" cried a small male voice. "Take your hand away, intruder!"

The Ken doll animated jerkily, then leaped upon Alandra's fingers, biting her thumb. With a shriek, Alandra grasped the doll by the torso, lifted it, and bashed it against the side of the dresser. Its head sheared off cleanly, bouncing away into the

shadows. Alandra tossed the body after it and
reached again for the mirror's pearl-inlaid handle.

"Oh, Kenny!" wailed the Barbie doll in grief.
The slim blond doll—who looked amazingly like
a diminutive Alandra—leaped at the princess's
face, scratching. Alandra batted the doll down
and jumped on top of it.

She grabbed the mirror, took a moment to as-
certain that yes, this was what she was looking
for, then turned to hightail it out of this decep-
tively innocuous but quite dangerous place.

But as she turned, the other dolls—dozens upon
dozens—came alive! Glass eyes sparkled and
gleamed. Molded bodies struggled up to staggered
stands and stumbled forward, arms outstretched,
sharp teeth flashing and gnashing. A Cabbage Patch
doll leaped and tore off a piece of her gown; a
toddler doll wet on her foot. Grasping her treasure firmly, she kicked a pair of GI Joes away,
then flung the lamp. It smashed in the midst of
the gathering dolls. Oil splashed, and flame spread
until the room was a conflagration of burning,
screaming dolls.

Alandra sprinted back to the main chamber,
where Herbivorous was still chasing Alabaster in
a spray of flung fur, snarls, and shrieks.

"Mistress!" the cat yeaked. With a burst of speed,
he leaped a full four yards from the top of a chair
into her arms. The force of the leap thrust Alandra
back. Her feet flew out from under her and she
landed square on her butt, a plush rug softening
her tumble only marginally. Mouth afoam, the
monstrous dog grasped opportunity and raced to
tear the fallen couple's throats out.

Automatically, Alandra lifted the mirror up to
defend herself.

Herbivorous halted in midrush, as though it had slammed into some invisible wall. It stared into the mirror, its eyes glazing over, its jaw slackening. It appeared hypnotized.

Alandra did not pause to question her good fortune. She removed Alabaster from her lap and raced for the door. The cat bounded at her heels and barely made it into the hall before Alandra slammed the door.

They both took some moments to regain their breath in the dark hallway. Alandra lifted the hand mirror and said, "Alley, there must be something very special about this mirror!"

"Yes," the cat returned, still wheezing from exertion. "It probably talks. Doesn't everything else?"

"It's my magic mirror, Alley!"

"What I want to know is why you tried to sacrifice me, your magic cat, to the magic dog!"

Clearly the cat was in a snit.

"We haven't time to argue, Alabaster. I think it would be wise to just save it till later and try to get out of here now. I just wish we had something to light our path with. I can't see anything!"

At that moment, the mirror came alight, casting out a diffuse lambent glow up and down the corridor.

"I think it likes you!" Alabaster said, awestruck despite himself.

"You see, Alley? You see why I had to have this delightful item? My intuition was true!"

Something crashed against the other side of the door. Frustrated barking emerged.

Alabaster screamed, "Yes, and your mother, too!" The cat executed a fruity Bronx cheer.

Alandra held her new light high and said, "Time

to go! I look forward to playing with my new
toy."

They struck off.

"Wasn't this a wonderful adventure, Alabaster?
Aren't you glad you came?"

"Why? I got nothing out of it!" the cat snarled
indignantly. "Where's my mirror? Where's my
toy? Cats like toys too, you know!"

Alandra was preoccupied with the tingling heat,
the coursing power she felt coming through the
handle of this delightful magical implement. What
glorious creature could possibly have made such
a delight?

She brought it down to examine it as best she
could as they walked down the hallway.

"How strange, Alley," she said. "The back of
the handle. It seems to be a collection of dice
faces!"

chapter thirteen

Ian Farthing could almost smell the things, even from the dark booth in which he sat.

He attempted to speak, but found fear clogging his throat. If it had been lighter in the booth, the others—involved now in conversation—would have noticed him shuddering, his face growing red as a beet, his eyes popping.

He twisted about again feverishly to make certain the peculiar lighting effects weren't playing tricks on his vision. Sure enough, there they still were like evil trunks newly sprouted from the beer-sopped floor: the Norx, as ugly a pair of beings as ever existed in sunlight. Ian's stomach flip-flopped at the thought of them riding hell-bent after Alandra, of Murklung, whom he had somehow defeated, and of how much his brothers would no doubt like to avenge him.

"Norx!" he managed explosively. "Norx!"

The others stopped their conversation. "Bless you, m'lad!" said the wyvern keeper.

"No," said Hillary, noting with alarm Ian's vexed state. "He's not sneezing. That's a much messier affair with Ian!"

"Don't look now, but there are Norx at the bar!" Ian said.

"Good Lord, lad," said Sir Godfrey. "Your impediment is back in triplicate!"

Ian tried again, but he spewed out incomprehensible garbage.

"Is he insulting Orcs?" said Thur, frowning.

"Something must be wrong," said Hillary. "Ian, try to speak slower."

"Here, lad. Cool off!" Godfrey splashed him with half a tankard of ale.

"Norx!" Ian spluttered. "The Norx! They'll get us for sure!"

"He's talking about Norx—they're the ones he saw pursuing the princess," Hillary said. "Norx at the bar."

The knights turned their attention that way. "Good grief," said Sir Oscar. "Nasty buggers, all right!"

Hands shot to sword hilts.

Their half-orc host took a glance, then said, "What's the fuss about, gentlemen? Norx are not uncommon visitors to Fisher's. They like their spot of tavern brew as much as any fantastic folk!"

Ian had calmed down enough to speak decipherably. "I recognize them, though. They're the ones!"

One of the Norx turned their way, and Ian's backbone seemed to freeze. Whimpering, he tried to duck under the table.

"My lad!" said Thur in reassuring tones. "All Norx look much the same!"

The Norx turned his head back and took a long swig from a gigantic mug.

"I don't care," said Ian, quivering beneath the

able, hiding his head. "That Norx is not going to see me!"

"My, you have a right little coward in your number," the keeper laughed. "Hardly quest material, it seems to me!"

"Farthing, you're embarrassing us!" said Sir Godfrey. He smiled over at the swarthy Thur. "Really, he can be quite brave if he is forced to be."

"Ian, do come out from under there," scolded Hillary. Godfrey gave him a good stiff boot in the ribs, and Ian scampered out, but kept his face hidden.

"You don't know . . . don't know what they're like. Awful! Awful!"

"And right he be," said Thur. "And a riled Norx is something to see! But these fellows are drinking, and a Norx on duty never drinks. Besides, take a look, young son. They're leavin'."

"Are you certain?" said Alison Gross, who had hidden her head in her arms as well. "I know Norx, and they'd just as soon spit you as spit at you!"

Ian ventured a glance. Sure enough, the hulking pair were skulking away, dead eyes thoroughly uninterested in searching out anything or anybody among the carousing crowd.

"There now," said the wyvern keeper. "Fears allayed? This is a haven, after all, for all sorts of questionable characters. I should be surprised if you didn't see a Norx or two quaffing a pint. Now then, I suspect you are tired. Let's drink up and I'll show you to my stables. We'll settle up the exchange of coinage and then you can be off with the dawn!"

"Don't we get some sort of flying lessons?" queried Sir Oscar doubtfully.

"Nay. The wyverns are good lads, and smart. They'll do the flying for ye! Just point them in the right direction, that's all."

Ian, still with the shakes, tried to steady himself with a final cup of beer, but all he got was indigestion.

By the time the knights had drunk their fill, the tavern had gotten even more crowded and raucous. An unbelievable din of dancing feet and singing voices filled the smoke-clogged atmosphere, and the company had to step over more than one snoring thug or dwarf on their way toward the exit.

And the streets seemed an extension of the besotted revelry of the Bar and Grail. Brawls and squawls and every imaginable type of crusty musty villain choked the byways. Ian had to step lightly to avoid the spills of vomit and hills of refuse that added their distinct odors to the general effluvium hazing the environs like fog.

Barkamus Thur guided them through crooked alleys and down cracked cobblestone to the edge of the city, where bushes and fields began to show.

In one of those fields, outlined by one of the luminous dice moons, a large barn seemed to thrust from the ground like a particularly large and splotchy bit of rectangular fungus.

"That's it!" cried Thur proudly. "There my babies lie o' nights. By day, I let 'em roam if they're not workin'. Difficult to handle a restless wyvern—damned difficult!"

They approached the building, and the keeper opened the hangar doors, beckoning the company to enter.

Sir Godfrey hesitated, peering into the dark gloom. "How do we know we're not walking directly into some wyvern's open jaws?"

"Oh, they're asleep back in their stables. Besides, they don't eat men." Thur guffawed at the very notion. "Do you think I could hire my babies out if they had a taste for their passengers? Bad business, Sir G." He lit a lantern and walked into the cavernous darkness first. "But if you've still doubts, come and take a look."

He guided the hesitant group back toward a series of fence stalls. The light fell upon dark forms sprawled and snoring on the straw-covered ground. Ian could make out long batlike wings folded along leathery hides. The place smelled of dust and offal, spiked with a strong lizard scent.

"I've got five of them, but you'll only need three," said the keeper. "Each of my babies can handle two passengers easily."

"Let's make that four," said Sir Godfrey, eyeing Alison Gross distastefully. "We've enough money, and our hag guide can have her own dragon steed."

"Please!" said Thur, scandalized. "These are not just ordinary dragons! They're wyverns!"

"What's the difference?" asked Hillary, fascinated.

The keeper cast an assaying glance upon her. "Of course, ye wouldn't know, would ye, being brought up outside the Circle. Well, granted, wyverns be dragons—but dragons of breeding, the real royalty as it were. None of your St. George runty worm stock, nor the sort that sits and rots atop treasure in some fathomless cavern. Nay, these beauties are descended, they say, from the beasts the demigods rode upon in the days of yore! They are beautiful beasts, as ye will see in

the mornin', and they fly like an angel's dream.
Swift and strong and sure, aye—and noble. Stead-
fast. Reliable. Else I should not be able to rent
them out to questers like ye."

"So what you're saying then is that these aren't
nasty dragons," said Hillary. "The type that steal
virgins and eat villages and stuff."

"No, they eat what I give them—and here I feed
them prime beef, not prime thief." He grinned.
"So, gentlemen, I charge ten pieces of gold per
wyvern for a week's hire—plus a healthy deposit
fully refundable upon your return."

Sir Godfrey cried, "What?" and entered into a
spirited and healthy dickering over the price.

When each party was satisfied that he had properly cheated the other, Barkamus accepted a small
additional sum for lodging and dragged out pal-
lets and blankets for their use.

The wyvern keeper promised to return in the
morning and teach the party the proper use of his
creatures. He then repaired to the small house in
the rear, which he assured them had only a single
bed.

Sir Oscar had doubts. "What if we're just supposed to be midnight snacks for these beasts?" he
grumbled as the wary travelers laid out their
bedsacks. "I don't care for a repeat of our troll
experience."

Alison Gross answered quickly, "I know these
wyverns well enough, and I can vouch for the
keeper's word and his honesty—at least in this
matter."

Sir William McIllvaine shifted uneasily in his
crouch on the straw, keeping his eye on the scaly
shadows bulking on the other side of the wood

fencing. "Still and all, I dislike the idea of sleepin' with them."

"I assure you, gentlemen!" said Alison. "These are not violent nor hungry creatures." Her hands reached for the button to her ragged blouse. "You want to look into my—"

"No, no. Belay that!" Sir Godfrey ordered. "I've heard of venting spleens, but this is a little much. No, I believe you, but still there's no reason not to keep a lookout, as is our usual practice."

Hillary waved her hand eagerly. "I'll be first. I'm not tired at all!"

"Very well," said Sir Godfrey, digging an hourglass out of his pack and handing it to the girl. "Two hours only, lass, then wake up Sir Bill here for the next shift, since he's so worried."

McIllvaine grumbled, but said nothing.

Within minutes, the weary travelers were bedded down and snoring, Ian eventually following after them.

But he had hardly seemed to snatch any rest at all when he woke up to the sound of two voices, one girlish, one gruff and snarly.

"So what happened then?" asked the girlish voice.

"So the prince says to the creature, 'What's a ghoul like you doing in a place like this?'" returned the raspy voice, with a hiss.

Laughter.

Now Ian recognized the girlish voice. It most certainly belonged to Hillary Muffin. But the source of the sibilant response was unknown.

In a trice he was up, dagger in hand, and scooting over to protect his friend.

A large form jerked in the shadows at his sudden movement. A long neck supporting a lengthy snout and webbed, pointed ears reared back with alarm.

"Don't worry, Wallace," said Hillary, "it's just my klutzy friend."

"Hillary!" said Ian, walking up to where she sat by the fence. "Are you okay?"

"Of course I'm okay, silly. I'm just talking to one of the dragons!"

"Wyvern, please," sniffed the long-necked creature in the shadows. "Do not make the same mistake with my brethren. We are a proud breed, you see."

"Sorry." She turned to Ian. "Ian, I want you to meet Wallace Wyvern the Third. Wally, this is my friend Ian Farthing I told you about."

The wyvern folded a wing forward and nodded its head in a stately bow. "A true pleasure to meet the friend of someone so fair and sweet!"

"Wally says we can fly on him!" Hillary said eagerly.

"Right," said the wyvern. "Getting a bit restless lying about here. Wouldn't mind a bit of adventure. Hillary mentioned something about saving a princess, and I haven't done that in a donkey's years!"

Ian backed away a bit from the rustle of scales, the hiss of possibly fiery breath. "Er—Hillary, however did you—get to know this fellow?"

"I was standing watch and he just asked me, quite nicely, who the heck we were. And I told him," Hillary said, sounding quite pleased with herself. "We've been having such a nice chat. I'm really glad you woke up, Ian. You can tell Wally much more about this whole business than I can."

Ian sighed and communicated the gist of the story—as much as he knew, anyway.

"Oh, jolly good show!" said the wyvern when Ian was finished. "An extraordinary set of circumstances! A dragoon's castle upon a peak! Why, of course you need us, and I anticipate this adventure very much. We wyverns have been getting such drudge work of late, and it will be very nice indeed to indulge in something exciting!"

"I can easily predict that you'll be getting a lot of excitement, now that things have gone quite ga-ga," Ian noted sarcastically.

"Oh, you mean twisting about and all that! Well, I suppose it's a bit cataclysmic, but you never know what to expect in a land of magic like this. And as old as I am, I've seen a few things to chill the bones, believe me!" The wyvern shuddered, and its wings and tail flapped spasmodically.

"Wallace says he used to roam free through the Circle," said Hillary.

"So why did you settle down with a sharpie like Barkamus?" Ian asked, surprised.

"Oh, he's not the first. Have to have someone as go-between, don't you know. Yes, we've transportation services to offer, we wyverns, and in return we get nice dry beds, good regular food, and a touch of adventure from time to time. What more could a civilized beastie possibly want?"

"Treasure?" Ian offered, his mind still firmly rooted in myth, picturing dragons aswim in piles of coin and jewels.

"Oh, our keeper throws the occasional bauble our way to satisfy certain atavistic urges. But you must realize that we are all rather old by your standards, and though physically we are quite suitable for work, emotionally we are in retirement."

"Sort of an old folks' home for wyverns, huh?"

Ian said. "But if you're so old, you must know a great deal about the Circle."

"Oh yes! And I've got a head full of reading and hearing a preposterous amount of legends and prophecies and such—one of which predicted just this sort of eschatology."

"Eschatology?" said Hillary. "Isn't that the study of escalators?"

"No, Hiller. It's the study of the End Times. You know, the Rapture, the Second Coming of Christ, the Judgment," Ian explained.

"Well now, it is if you're stuck in the Judeo-Christian mythos!"

"Oh, but with Celtic spices and whole chunks of Norse flavorings!" Hillary said.

"We've got quite a different kettle of stew here, my dear," said Wally. "One of the central legends of the Dark Circle is that it's a bit of a mixing bowl of worlds. So by all means keep the faith, but remember that God wears many masques!"

Ian felt his interest pricked. "Can you tell us any more about these prophecies? Perhaps you can tell us something about why Alandra is so important!"

"Yes!" piped Hillary, excited. "From the sounds of it, she seems to merely be a rather nasty girl!"

"Hmm. This Key you spoke of . . . naturally, I have heard of Alandra. The deceased Bellworthy's daughter, no? Key, you say she is called. Which of course implies a lock, which in turn should be attached to some sort of door. . . ."

Great green orbs blinked in the lamplight as the wyvern considered. Suddenly a gust of wind came from the distended purple nostrils ending its snout, and its spiky antennae quivered. "The Portal, of course. The fabled Portal!"

"Pardon?" Ian said.

"Oh, of course, you're probably not aware of that particular story," said Wally, drawing nearer and lowering his voice as though this was a matter of confidential material. "One of our creation myths—and we've got a few, let me tell you, being such a conglomerate here in the Dark Circle—states that when God created the Circle, he also created a pathway to Heaven, or at least to the land where He lived—a pathway bounded at this end by a door . . . the Portal. However, not only is the location of this Portal a secret, but the Portal is locked."

"And Alandra is the Key to this mystical Portal?" said Ian. "But why would evil creatures wish access to a corridor that leads to God?"

"You must recall that this is myth—and perhaps the word 'God' can be interpreted as 'power.' So maybe these fellows—and I am quite aware of their reps, believe you me, Morgsteen in particular—see access to this Portal as a way to obtain power over the Circle."

The wyvern smiled with self-satisfaction—a dreadful sight with its fangs gleaming, eyes twinkling, and antennae crinkling.

"Fascinating," said Ian. "A Gateway to God!" Something tingled inside of him—a shiver touched the base of his bent spine. Outwardly he had always resented the Powers That Were . . . but the prospect of actually coming head to Godhead with them filled him with a kind of wonder. A distant event, surely, but nonetheless a light at the end of the tunnel, a bright star in a black turbulent sky, a mystic reality at the end of a long sequence of mixed metaphors.

"Well, I've got a thing or two to tell God," said Hillary in a bluff tone.

"Mind you, my new acquaintances," said the wyvern, "these are but legends. Truth is often much more complex and certainly much stranger!"

"But what of yourself?" said Ian. "We would surely like to hear more of your history."

"Later! Later, certainly!" said the wyvern. "We'll have a full day tomorrow, so we should get some rest."

Hillary yawned and stretched. "Yes, Ian. I should get some sleep. Would you be a dear and take watch for a while?"

Ian's mind was racing too quickly to sleep anyway, so he assented. As human and wyvern feet trod and rustled back to sleeping places, Ian took up his post by the lamp. His thoughts ranged out beyond the light and beyond the darkness to the halls of Heaven itself.

Why did the notion enthrall him so? he wondered as he wound a piece of straw around a forefinger absently. The idea of entering through this fabled Portal grabbed at something very deep and essential in his soul. . . .

Could it possibly have something to do with who he really was? Could the secret of his origin lie beyond that door? Could he solve the mystery of a little boy who fell from the sky into Mullshire?

No, he concluded. Probably not. But he had to check it out anyway, just in case.

This concluded, he promptly began to drowse, dreaming of celestial choirs voicing Ave Diems among mist and stars and cloudy climes.

He awoke to the sound of whispers, of the hangar doors opening, of shuffling footsteps and a hissing torch. Horses whinnied in their stalls.

"Right," a voice said. "Here they be, as promised. Now pay before ye do your dirty deeds."

His vision focused.

Dimly lit, three figures stood on the threshold of the barn.

One was Barkamus Thur.

The other two were stout things, barrellike bodies dominating the surroundings.

"Your payment," said a gravelly voice, "is this."

A sword lifted.

"Nice workmanship," said Thur. "But haven't you got cash? And remember, I get their stuff!"

The sword flashed.

The entrepreneur's head flew from his shoulders on a gush of blood. It landed in Ian's lap, surprised eyes still staring.

"Nice catch," it said, and then died.

"Norx!" Ian wailed frantically, tossing the head away. "Norx! We've been betrayed!"

Sir Godfrey was the first to his feet. "What are you wailing incomprehensibly about now, dammit?"

Ian pointed a bloody finger at the huge figures blocking the way out, their blades glimmering in the lamplight.

"Oh," said Godfrey. "Yes, indeed. Norx. They are rather fierce-looking, aren't they, Farthing?" His voice changed to a scream. "To arms!"

In total disarray, the others erupted to their feet and drew their weapons, noticeably quavering at the sight of these mammoth killers and the sprawled and bloody body of their host.

"The Lady Alandra," said one. "In the name of His Highness Morgsteen, where is she?"

"Whew," said Sir Godfrey, holding his nose. "Haven't you guys heard of deodorant?"

"Alandra!" the other bellowed.

"She's at Lord Princerik's Keep on Scabrous Peak in the Mystique Mountains!" wailed Alison Gross, falling to her knees. "Mercy, oh mercy, minions of Morgsteen!"

"Damn ye!" cried Sir Godfrey. "Spilled the beans. Well, that just means these noxious creatures will have to be destroyed before they can relay that bit of news." He waved his sword airily. "Ian, why don't you just flick out your pen and write them off? There's a good lad!"

"Me!" Ian said, fumbling for his weapon. "Why always me?"

"We'll keep this one occupied," said Sir Godfrey, indicating the closest Norx, "while you carve up the other. En garde, fiend!"

Sir Godfrey grabbed Sir Oscar and Sir William and flung them toward Toothmaw.

Swords changed and banged. The knights groaned with effort and were hard pressed to keep their foe at bay.

Ian found the pen in his pocket. He pulled it out.

"Oh, Ian," cried Hillary. "Be careful!"

Ian Farthing held his small weapon out and took a deep breath. "Stand back, villain!" he said in a deep and resonant voice that surprised even him. "Begone or feel the taste of the Pen That Is Mightier Than the Sword!"

The Norx looked at one another, shrugged, and continued fighting. "We shall send you all to Hell!" grunted one. "Thus will Alandra's mortal succor fail, and your quest be broken!"

"Impossible!" Ian said, his mind full of legend from his talk with Wally the Wyvern. "Our quest is holy! So feel the sting of holy steel, you foul creatures."

He pushed the button of his pen. Again, a blade shot from it, trembling with dazzles. Again, his arms grew in proportion and dimension. Feeling the power fill his head giddily, Ian stepped forward only slightly scared out of his skull this time.

The Norx called Tombheart lunged. Sparks flew as his blade touched Ian's.

Ian staggered to one side with the incredible force of the blow, off balance.

The Norx picked a stone ax from his belt.

"Rock bashes steel!" it grunted as it swung the weapon around, grazing Ian on the noggin.

Ian Farthing promptly saw stars and dropped onto his face in the straw.

chapter fourteen

The magus fell.

How long he'd been falling by the time he regained consciousness, he could not tell. Not long, probably, though a look upward did not spot the house and space/time island from which he'd tumbled.

Around him passed stars and planets in their precise but now unreadable astrological orderings. Below was a great well of darkness, which would consume him, eventually—and spew him out where?

There were still mysteries piled upon enigmas, even to Crowley Nilrem.

His fall seemed more of a drifting; it owned a timeless quality, like lying half awake in a bed of space, with the stars for sheets. He knew that if he surrendered, his mind would be lost in the vastness of it all, and soon his body would become star-stuff again.

"No!" he cried, and the solidity of the word dragged his awareness back into its central point behind his eyes, within his skull.

While he was yet alive and conscious, there was hope. While he yet clung to the Eyes, he had a chance. Slowly and carefully as he tumbled down head over heels, he found his pocket and pulled the pair of Destiny Dice from their place snuggled in his pocket. The Eyes of Ivory. Their firmness in his palm, the touch of their depthless magic, caused a surge of confidence to enter him once more.

Colin Rawlings must be stopped, and that lot fell to him. That the powerful wizard thought Nilrem was fallen to his doom was an advantage, but only if Nilrem could avert that doom.

He stared "down" again, hopeful. But his hope was instantly dashed. He had not fallen toward the maelstrom of the Dark Circle, the direction in which he had thrown his cat Alabaster, and no amount of flailing or tacking or space-swimming could change his course.

"Oh, Dice, oh Eyes," he said aloud. "What shall I do?" He clutched the pair of ivories close and tried to remember an appropriate incantation.

One came to him instantly; he was so shocked at its nature, his mind rebelled at the thought of using it. Desperately, he tried to remember some other spell, some other curse even, but none had sufficient power.

No, he would have to use the Surrender Song.

Clutching the dice close to his heart, he began to chant:

"To a great force I take my course,/ to the ultimate source I make my plea./ To a Power that is Greater I tender in surrender/ My soul for the Good I devote the light that is me."

He cringed at the very sound of the words, and had particular trouble forcing out the last verse. Crowley Nilrem for the Good! An abomination! The Gaming Magi were, like the Fates, neither good nor evil, though those qualities were used in their elaborate games. They were Above All That, after all—they were the Prime Manipulators, intellectual expressions of cosmic principles. They served themselves, not good or evil.

But Nilrem, falling, was desperate.

And as the last syllable of the Surrender Song left his lips, he knew that if he survived this, he would be a servant of Truth and Law and Good.

How dreadfully dull.

Still, he thought, consider the alternative. . . .

Almost immediately, he felt a rush of something electric. The dice in his hand felt warm. He opened his fingers and saw that they glowed with an unearthly pearlescence.

He felt a dizzy loss of self, and something very much like grateful emotion swept through him.

He found that there were tears in his eyes.

That wasn't so bad, he thought, surprised. It was actually quite fulfilling in a straightforward way.

Abruptly, something flashed in front of him.

Something fluttered against his cheek.

He grabbed it. It was a tarot card . . . one of his pack that had fallen with him!

Nilrem turned it over and instantly recognized the sign.

It was the queen of wands.

His mother!

Well, if it had to be, it had to be—though she wouldn't care much for his new alignment with Truth and Good.

With no further hesitation, he held the card out before him, concentrating on its image—a woman in royal apparel clutching a set of batons. His tumbling slowed, then stopped altogether. He hung in space, the universes twinkling about him like an infinite jewelry display.

Then he voiced the spell—and instantly his celestial site dissolved away, first to total darkness, and then . . .

He was standing in dusk, cement beneath his feet, the blare of horns in his ears. Beyond the taxis and cars that rolled down the city avenue, trees rustled in autumn breezes. A man in a trenchcoat walked past him, a copy of the *New York Times* tucked under an arm.

Crowley Nilrem blinked.

He backed up against the stone side of a building, feeling faint, getting his bearings.

The right-angled sign on the corner stated that this was the intersection of Central Park West and 88th Street. So, Mother was staying in New York now. What a gadabout! Of course, with her money and powers, she could afford to be. The question that Crowley Nilrem had was why she insisted on staying on this quite tedious world with its dull, uniform people and its technology mania. Even though he'd been born here, he still couldn't retain any kind of fondness for the place.

The air was full of automobile fumes, garbage odor, and the smell of dog crap. Nilrem coughed, righted himself (whew, he hated the smell of Manhattan! Thank God, Mother didn't live in New Jersey!), and mustered what dignity he could, considering that he looked like a refugee from a Salvation Army soup kitchen of the nineteenth century. He walked down 88th, hoping that Mother had some new clothes that would fit him.

Mother's brownstone was quite close to Columbus Avenue, and he noted immediately that the area had undergone a good deal of gentrification since he'd last trod these sidewalks. He noted new stores on Columbus, a new condo displaying the sign NOW SELLING. He sneaked a peak around the corner, and saw that his favorite diner was still open, down on 85th. The people who paced the sidewalks now, though, were of a much higher social background than the last time Nilrem had been here.

Well, well, well, he thought. At least not everything is disintegrating.

He found the brownstone's address, checked the name by the buzzer just in case (Mrs. Ernestine Bennett . . . yes, that was Mother's incarnation here, though by no means her real name), then hit the button.

He had to repeat this twice before a voice rattled the metal grate: "Yes? Hello, who's there?"

"It's Crowley, Mother," he said.

"Who?"

Damn. She never would get his new name right.

"It's Potty Pie, Mother. You know. Elmore. Your darling snoogums son?"

"Potty Pie! How darling of you to visit! Let me just ring you in. Let me see if I can . . . still haven't mastered this contraption, and I've given Brixton the night off. . . ."

The door buzzed.

"There, Potty, now open the door and come on up. I'm on the top floor, dear. Don't dawdle, please!"

Crowley Nilrem grabbed the doorknob, twisted, and entered. There was another door at the end of the foyer, but it was unlocked.

He took a deep breath and entered his mother's home, wondering what he was in for this visit.

He prayed that Mother had gotten rid of those pets of hers. True, demons made great watchdogs, especially in a town like New York City, but they had difficulty differentiating between friendly visitors and burglars; Crowley just didn't have either the magic, the strength, or patience to deal with a batdog or a werecat roaring up to him.

But nothing detained him from climbing the first two flights of steps.

Mother had once more changed her furniture, he could see from the brief glimpses of her living and drawing rooms. Where once she had had elegant antiques, now there were spare white and black and gray blocks of modern furniture, hunkered over by sleekly designed lamps and planters.

But the third floor was different, he saw as its door creaked open to him.

Here felt more like home, with the smells of ancient books and antique wax, the wisps of old spice and perfume from Egypt or Abyssinia, perhaps; and the pervading touch of tingly feminine magic, like static electricity in drag.

In the distance, Chinese chimes tinkled. A faint melody from an old record player sweetened the air: "Moon River."

"Mother!" Crowley Nilrem called. "Mother, I'm here."

One entire wall of the room was filled with old books and boxes. A coffee table held no fewer than four crystal balls of various sizes. On a card table was a deck of the tarot, half-told. A cigar lay dead in an ashtray, half-smoked, its memory strong in the atmosphere. Mother and her Cuban bombers, Nilrem thought, shaking his head.

Beads clacked behind him: someone moving through the partition.

Nilrem spun on his heel.

His mother stood there, aghast.

"Darling," she said. "You look . . . awful!"

She had the faint lines of an older woman in her strongly angled face. But, of course, she was much older than your normal old woman. Her hair was newly permed; its gray-touched brunette rolled about in elaborate waves. She wore a blue evening dress.

"I told you," Nilrem said. "I'm involved in a crisis of immense proportions!"

"Oh yes, of course. You did call last week . . . or was it yesterday? I hope my advice was worthwhile. How is dear Dunworthy?" She was busy touching on droplets of a subtle French perfume.

"Dead, Mother!" Nilrem said impatiently. "And his body is possessed by none other than Colin Rawlings!"

"That little brat is back! Why, I paddled his little bum more than I can remember when he was a tyke." She sniffed, and put the cap back in the bottle. "Clearly it didn't do any good!"

"Mother," said Nilrem, exasperated. "He's got the other magi frozen in some kind of stasis spell."

"Why, clever fellow! Do go on, but make it fast. Baryshnikov is dancing tonight at the ballet, and you know how I adore that risqué Russian's tight little buns!" Mischievous lights danced in her pale-blue eyes.

"He almost killed me, Mother!"

She paused at that and looked at him sternly. "Really, I know that boys must have their fun, but don't you think that you and your crew are taking all this business a little too seriously, Sydney?"

"My name is Crowley now, Mother," he said, clenching his teeth to keep from yelling. "The fate of this universe, all the universes, hangs in the balance. If Rawlings gets hold of the Key to the God of Games ... well, I just shudder at the thought!"

Mrs. Bennett shrugged. "Things have been quiet hereabouts. I've got a few quite handy demons I can summon up to help you out. How would that be, Andrew?"

"Mother, no demons. I can't ... I've ... I've had to throw in with the Forces of Good to save my tail."

Fire flared in the woman's eyes for a moment—and then she looked closely at the magus.

"Just don't invite any of that stinking crowd to any of my tea socials, hear?" she said.

"Invite? How could I?" Nilrem retorted. "They generally get crucified or stoned or stuck with arrows if they go public."

"And you won't go public?"

"Mother, I had to save my hide! I have to stop Rawlings! The Circle is in total chaos!"

Mother pouted for a moment, then relented. "Well, I hope it doesn't last."

"It doesn't have to last, Mother!" Nilrem said eagerly. "There's hope for the Circle—and your favorite Gaming Magus."

"Really. Boys and their sandbox wargames!" She went to a mirror and inspected her makeup.

"Oh, I hate to grovel!" Nilrem said, clenching his fists. "I hate to act the child for you, Mother. But I have no choice. I need your help, your wisdom—Mother, you've always come through for me!"

The regal lady examined her son appraisingly. "Ever since you were a tyke, you've always loved your games, Sydney. And ever since you discovered that the biggest game of all was Reality, there's been no stopping you. Now, I will admit you've played very cleverly. After all, you are my son, and I've taught you well in those earthly cosmic matters in which I am versed. But I've limited my Reality, son, and that is part of my strength, and that is why you've come running here, isn't it? There is solidity here, a place upon which to stand, or rest or whatever, before you sally forth once more into the fray. But even if you do triumph over this awkward situation, you're going to have to realize that it's time to grow up, Sydney. It's time to choose your place to stand. The gods are not the lucky ones—and after all, what are Gaming Magi but ludicrous infants aspiring to godhood?"

"The name is Crowley, now, Mother, and there won't be any place to stand if I don't do something soon!"

"Very well. What do you need?" She examined her diamond watch wearily. "I have a half hour, I suppose, so make it fast!"

"Oh, Mother, I do love you!" He stepped over and kissed her on the cheek. "First of all, a new set of clothes—"

"No problem. And I suppose that you'll want to be sent back to wake up your other magi friends!"

"No," said Crowley Nilrem. "That would be much too dangerous. Besides, even if I did, times are such that I'm not sure that it would do any good at all. No, I have to take matters into my own hands."

"How do you propose to do that?"

"Mother, I mentioned that Rawlings has made a complete carnage of the Circle. Claims to be redoing his particular design, though God knows how. Well, he can cause the Circle to reform into a hula hoop or a horseshoe if he bloody chooses to—but he can't change the basic principles of its function without getting the correct materials from the God of Games, who helped collaborate on the original rules."

"Gads! That clown!" sniffed his mother. "Rawlings always amused me, but that turkey is simply insufferable!"

"Don't worry, Mother. No tea for him. But let me finish. There is a princess in the dark circle who has the power to open the Portal to God Avenue . . . the one They sealed off millennia ago."

"In disgust, no doubt, with the antics of you spoiled brats!"

"Be that as it may," Nilrem said, trying to retain his poise and sense of dignity, but failing, "she is up for grabs, loose in the Dark Circle. If Colin Rawlings gets hold of her power to open that Portal—well, there could very well be another collaboration, and goodness knows what would come about then! Who knows? Perhaps no more ballet!"

"Barbaric!" Mrs. Bennett said, becoming interested. "What do you propose to do?"

"The struggle focuses down to a more physical, less esoteric level at this point, I think," said Nilrem emphatically. "I must somehow transport myself down to the Circle of this princess, and make sure that her power is not used for wrong . . . by whomever!"

"There are others who are in line?"

"Oh, yes, and that, I fear, is the fault of us Gaming Magi. We helped invent characters of pure ridiculous, almost fictional, cunning and evil who crave power and realize that they might obtain it through control of the princess. Perhaps we are children, Mother, to have perpetrated such madness. Pathetic little children!"

"This could be dangerous, then."

"Oh yes, for I would be vulnerable to all kinds of physical hurt. But I still know my spells you taught me, Mother. And I was very high on my wizard level, as you may recall."

"Cripes, do I! You and that Celtic hunk almost clobbered the Saxons. But then you had to let that sorcerous wench imprison you!"

"Part of the game, Mother. But that was so primitive . . . this is much more complex, much more cosmic. At any rate, what I need from you is help in transporting me back to the Circle. But not just anywhere. I know where this princess is now. We Gaming Magi had just located her when we were so crudely interrupted."

"And you want me to ship you back there?"

"If you would."

She smiled, and nodded. "But do me a favor, Crowley. Don't do too many good deeds. It will wreck our family's reputation."

"I wouldn't dream of it, dearest Mother," said Crowley, clutching nervously at the dice in his pocket, hoping fervently that he had made the right choice.

"I ask but one favor in return, Crowley."

"Anything!"

"If you succeed you'll come and spend some

time with me. There are some lovely women I
want you to meet. It's time for you to think about
getting married and settling down!''

Crowley Nilrem sighed. "Yes, Mother.''

chapter fifteen

When Ian Farthing crumpled after his knock on the head, the others were upset, to say the least, with Sir Godfrey Pinkham the most put-out by this turn of events.

"Farthing!" the knight cried, sidestepping to the fallen fellow. "You can't do this!" Godfrey kicked the lad in the side, but obtained no response. "Dammit, you can't leave us in the lurch like this!"

This, of course, was not Ian Farthing's point of view. Ian's point of view was total obliviousness.

The Norx brandished their swords, which shone silver-gold-blood in the lamplight. In a spray of saliva and bad breath, Tombheart expounded his position in the bargaining: "Take us to Queen Alandra, or we will slice you all into lunchmeat!"

"A pox on you!" Godfrey cried. "She is a princess, she is no queen!"

"She is queen to our Lord Morgsteen," said Toothmaw, advancing a step, pointing his sword at Godfrey. "And it is our duty to bring her back to his castle."

"Damn your eyes, you'll do no such thing!" Godfrey leaned down and wrested the pen from

Ian's grasp. "Remove your foul carcasses," he cried, "or face the fury of this powerful magic!"

"You wish to sign your death certificate?" said Tombheart, clearly puzzled.

But Godfrey's efforts to cause the device to grow into a sword proved fruitless. Desperately, he gazed down upon Ian's fallen form. There, in his belt, was the strange sword the guy claimed he'd won from a Norx. Godfrey drew it out. "Careful, there, foul things! We have met with your kind before, and see our prize!"

All four Norx eyes widened perceptibly. "The weapon of Murklung!" growled one. "Vengeance!" ground out the other.

"This is supposed to discourage you!" Godfrey said, clearly disappointed. "Well, come then," he cried, bracing himself. "And taste steel."

"I think they prefer blood," said Sir Oscar.

Alison Gross was cowering in the corner, but she seemed to finally take heart. "This is all unnecessary!" she said. "No one needs to die. I can take you to Alandra. We can ride the wyverns."

"Alison!" said Hillary. "Don't betray us!"

"Betray you?" The hag seemed honestly grieved at the thought. "I'm trying to save you. You do not know the fighting power of the Norx. You will all die, and they will force me to take them to Alandra anyway."

"But surely you would refuse!" Sir Godfrey said. "Surely you would not throw in with these scoundrels!"

"I would if my life depended on it, honey," Alison said. "Best you believe that. Besides, what do I care as long as I get back to the Keep and someone takes that witch away from my Princerik?"

"It is of no consequence," said Toothmaw. "We

must kill the keepers of our brother's sword, anyway!" The Norx advanced steadily upon Sir Godfrey, who held the weapon up defiantly.

Hillary knelt down by Ian. "Wake up!" she demanded, shaking him. "Wake up, Ian!"

His response was a snore.

"Come, fellows!" said Sir Godfrey, gesturing to his knights. "If we must die, let us die bravely!" He motioned for a charge, but as Sir Mortimer, Sir William, and Sir Oscar ran forward, he paused just long enough to make sure that they were first. "Let us show these hellspawn the courage of good Christian knights."

Immediately, the barn erupted into the chaos of clanging swords, shouts, and grunts as metal flailed like short bursts of lightning. The knights fought well, and coordinated as a team they cut and thrust and drew the odd bit of greenish blood from Norx hides. But under the fierce Norx attack, they fell back little by little.

"Psst! Hillary Muffin!" cried a voice from behind the girl, somehow cutting through the terrible din.

Hillary Muffin spun and saw the head of Wallace Wyvern craning over the top of the gate.

"Wally!" she cried, hurrying to him. "Your keeper is dead, and the Norx—"

"Shhh!" the wyvern said. "Yes, I saw. Poor Barky. The chums and I are a bit upset. Still, the fellow was a scoundrel and earned what he got."

"You've got to help us!" Hillary cried.

"Well, now, we wyvern know from experience not to tangle with Norx. Just the thing to get our wings clipped." The light from the lamps glittered in its jewellike eyes as it turned toward the battle raging now in its kennel. "But the blokes and I have discussed the matter, and if you can get your friends on top of us, we'll go out the back way!"

Hillary did not waste time discussing the offer. Immediately, she kissed the wyvern on its scaly cheek and ran to where Sir Godfrey directed the battle, holding a wounded arm.

"The wyverns!" she cried. "They'll take us!"

Alison Gross, upon hearing this, wasted no time in racing for the stalls and opening the gates.

"But should we turn our backs," said Sir Godfrey, "the Norx will make short work of us!"

Indeed, the Norx were pressing the tired knights, all nicked and cut, backward.

"You've got to wake Ian up!" said Sir Godfrey grimly. "I hate to admit this, but he's our only hope!"

"Give me back the pen, then," Hillary demanded. "He needs the pen."

"Yes, of course." Sir Godfrey handed over the strange and magical instrument.

Hillary rushed back and inserted the Pen That Is Mightier Than the Sword between Ian's fingers.

"Ian Farthing," she said, "you read me a story once that said that a man is the author of his own life." She took a deep breath and shook him hard. "Well, write, damm it!"

Ian Farthing was somewhere else, having a fascinating conversation.

"What difference does it make, anyway?" he asked, lounging comfortably in a hammock, sipping a long cool drink. "I mean, if I die, I die, and either I continue onward with my immortal soul, or I don't. I tried my best. I wasn't a bad person. What more can be asked of me?"

About him shifted clouds laced with rainbows. Sunlight limned golden edges and vapor misted up from nowhere like delightful slow-motion fountains. There was a feeling of finality about everything, a texture of eternity.

It was all rather like lying in a nice comfy bed in the middle of a sunny gilded morning, knowing you didn't have to get up until you pleased.

The person Ian Farthing was talking to was a young man he had met before—where, though, he did not know.

"Oh, come off it, Ian!" the young man said, hands on hips. "I've heard this kind of nonsense before. Look, it was this kind of innocent ignorance that got you into trouble from the beginning! 'Oooooh,' says the stalwart hero, 'I've had enough of this strenuous business. I think I'll join a choir or something and just sing the rest of my days.' Well, poppycock, my lad! You were born for trouble, and you love it, and you know it! It attracts you, and you attract it, so you might as well live up to your basic nature, because that's your destiny, bucko!"

A girlish voice sounded through the sky—a repetition of the urgent cry that had gotten this irksome conversation underway. "Ian! Ian, you must wake up!"

"Oh, drat," said Ian Farthing.

"That sounds to me like Hillary, Ian," said the young man, inspecting his manicure. "Are you truly going to let the dear girl down? And what of Alandra?"

Ian sat up from the hammock.

"What I want to know is, why can't someone else come to the rescue? Why me? Why not you, for instance?"

"Now, Ian, you know very well the answer to that question, so why even ask?"

And Ian did know, then, and realized he'd known, deep down, all along.

The young man smiled archly. "But of course, you won't be permitted to retain that knowledge up there. Which is just as well, because it would just make things confusing. Besides, it would take all the fun out of life!"

"Fun," said Ian sarcastically. "Oh yes, loads of fun."

"Wake up, Ian," said the young man. "Give it another go." Reaching over, the fellow tipped the glass over, spilling cold liquid in Ian's face.

Though in the waking world no water had been dumped on him, Ian Farthing spluttered awake.

He was instantly aware of Hillary's fingers on his face.

"Ian!" she said. "Your sword's in your hand. You must use it, or all is lost!"

He sat up, dripping straw. Sure enough, in his hand was the magic pen. Coming for him, déjà vu doubled, were the Norx pair, pushing back the knights, who fought them valiantly.

Before he even had time to consider, Ian held the pen out and pushed in its stud. With a flash of light, the sword grew into a mighty blade—but once more the nimbus traveled farther than the hilt, spreading up over Ian's arms, and this time washing over his whole body.

With a flash of coruscation, he changed into a well-muscled, handsome, blond-haired youth, flashing of eye, dashing in apparel. Hillary and Sir Godfrey stepped back in awe. Even the Norx blinked and lost ground before this dazzling change, shielding their eyes and barely preventing themselves from being stuck by Sir Mortimer and Sir Oscar, who seemed to be gaining their second breaths.

But inside, Ian still felt like himself, albeit certainly much less clumsy.

No time to ponder this good fortune, though, he knew. Immediately sensing his advantage, he hurled himself forward at the Norx, crying to the knights, "Out of the way!"

"To the wyverns!" Sir Godfrey cried, weighted down by the saddlebags he had just remembered to recover. "Ian will cover our retreat!"

The panting, beleaguered knights needed no encouragement, scampering away from the sword-bearing monsters and heading back to the stables.

"God bless you, Ian!" Hillary cried as she swung the gate open for the knights.

Swinging his sword in a wide swath, Ian Farthing advanced confidently. After all, he reasoned, every time he'd used the pen before, he'd won the battle. What a glorious sight he must present! He only wished he had a mirror.

"Ah, the magic sword again!" said Toothmaw, breaking his usual dead expression with a grin, lifting up the stone ax.

"I need a new toothpick!" Tombheart cried, jumping forward, clearly recovered from his surprise at Ian's metamorphosis.

Ian had rather hoped that his attack would be more impressive, but had no choice but to carry through. He aimed a blow at Toothmaw, since he was closest.

The Norx quickly parried the blow. Ian's arm seemed to vibrate painfully. He stepped back, and Tombheart pressed in, blade held high.

"You're supposed to be vanquished!" Ian cried,

jumping back to avoid the blow. "This is the Pen That Is Mightier Than the Sword!"

"Perhaps, foolish one," said Toothmaw, "but we do not read!" He aimed a thrust at Ian, which the lad avoided with an agility that he had never owned before.

Lithely, Ian leaped about and took a quick cut at Tombheart, which drew blood. He backpedaled as the Norx grunted with surprise. Toothmaw waved his stone ax, and Ian's bump on his head throbbed. He ducked just in time to avoid another blow.

Even with his magic sword, even with his increased agility, Ian was hard pressed to contain these creatures. They were startlingly quick for monsters, clearly highly skilled in the vocation of killing. Still, his duty now was not necessarily to destroy them—though that would be convenient—but to hold them back while the others boarded the wyverns.

His sword clanged and vibrated as it fended off another blow of the ax—for some reason, it seemed not as powerful in the presence of a stone weapon—and Ian was forced back a step. His heel touched metal on the ground—the Norx sword he had won from Murklung. Quickly, he bent, found the hilt, and brought it up with his left hand, with a surprising ease that testified to his increased strength.

"I killed your brother," he shouted, "and I killed his hand!"

Toothmaw and Tombheart looked at each other in astonishment.

"And I can certainly kill you!" he screamed, working up to a berserker rage, preparing for an onslaught.

"Ian!" he heard Hillary's voice cry out behind him. "Ian, we're ready!"

Ian looked back and saw wings stretching in preparation for flight from the stable; beyond was an outline of a door through which came the twinkling of stars.

Toothmaw took the opportunity of Ian's distraction to advance, swinging both his weapons.

Ian hit the ground, lunging forward. The point of the Norx sword caught Toothmaw in the lower leg. The Norx howled and fell, yanking the weapon from Ian's hand. Tombheart had been rushing forward as well; he stumbled over his fallen companion, falling face forward into the dirt with a terrible "OOOFFF!"

Ian saw his opportunity. He scrambled up and dashed back to the stables as the Norx struggled to regain their feet, Toothmaw groaning with pain, Tombheart cursing in some ancient language.

Already, Ian could see winged dragons outlined against the starlit sky. He hurried to the one lingering wyvern. "Ian!" called Hillary, perched on its leathery back. "Hop on!"

Ian needed no further encouragement. He mounted the wyvern, clinging to the rudimentary saddle and then swiveling about to protect the flank from the Norx.

But the creatures were still fighting to regain their feet, bashing and thrashing at each other in frustration as they saw their quarry about to escape.

"All on?" Wallace asked.

"Yes," said Hillary. "Hurry."

The wyvern bounded out into the night, spreading wings as it ran. Wind caught the wings and those great batlike limbs flapped away, lifting them up into the sky with a sickening lurch.

As the wyvern tilted in flight, Ian fought to hang on. The saddle was fitted with stirrups and handholds, but these seemed very useless as the flying creature rose up farther and farther in the sky. Ian fought dizziness and nausea—but all in all, he considered, it was better than getting hacked to death by the Norx.

When the wyvern leveled off, high into the night, Ian took time for a breath and noticed that his magic pen was back in its original form. He stuck it into a pocket for safekeeping and reasserted his grip.

Ahead flapped the four other wyverns, all bearing passengers.

"The one with Alison is in the lead," Hillary explained in a voice barely above the wind sounds sweeping over them. "She'll guide us all to the dragoon's Keep. Are you all right, Ian?" She twisted around to get a good look at him by the light of the rising moon.

"No wounds," he said.

"You've changed again, Ian," she said, turning around in place, her voice quieting. "Changed. . . ."

Changed? That was okay, thought Ian, as long as that change didn't necessitate getting buried.

The wyvern flapped onward toward dawn.

chapter sixteen

Ian Farthing had never flown before—as far as he knew.

"Oh, it's a grand life, the flying life," Wallace cried out just as day pinked the edges of the coiled world of the Dark Circle. "I've always quite enjoyed it!"

The wyvern banked playfully, though not steeply enough to cause his riders any danger.

"I think I prefer the groundling sort of existence," Ian Farthing commented, still hanging on for his life as they skimmed the top of a cumulus cloud.

Hillary Muffin said nothing. She had been quiet since she had commented on Ian's further changing.

And changed he was—Ian knew that even without a mirror. For one thing, he had felt his face and found it notably smoother, more even than before. But more important, he felt different—less gawky, more self-confident, even if he was a mile up in the air with nothing more between him and death than a hotdogging lizard with wings.

The other wyverns and their riders were in a staggered pattern in front of Wally, heading for the edge of another section of the coil. There rose a series of high-peaked mountains; Alison apparently was guiding the head wyvern well.

"Not a terribly long trip," Wallace said. "Hardly had time to get my wings limbered up."

"Glad you're up for long distance," said Ian. "But frankly, this is more than enough for me. Right, Hillary?" Ian was more than slightly astonished at the good mood he was in, after a lifetime of dragging about, feeling sorry for himself.

"Yes," she said, mopily.

"Hey!" he said, giving her a warm squeeze with a free hand. "What's wrong with Mistress Brightness and Cheer? We got through the worst of it, and now we're winging our way cheerily toward our destination on a friendly wyvern."

"Yes, toward wonderful Princess Alandra," said Hillary sarcastically. "Well, I suppose you're right, Ian, but I just can't get excited about meeting this delightful morsel of femininity."

Ian didn't know what to say to that.

"I'm sorry, Ian," Hillary apologized. "You're quite right, and I'm being awful. I guess I just can't get over not liking this woman!"

"Princesses do tend to be more trouble than they're worth," commented Wallace. "And from the sounds of it, this one's a right one!"

"But the important thing," Ian emphasized, "is that this part of our quest is a success."

He watched the horizon eagerly for sign of their destination.

Eventually, it reared before them, unmistakable: a castle atop a steep mountain, rising up from a sea of mist like some mystic isle.

The wyverns ahead drifted down toward it like leaves floating toward the ground.

"A very nice runway," noted Wallace as the other wyverns one by one swooped down to perfect three-point landings in the courtyard. Their mount made a similarly graceful spiraling plummet, and landed without too many jarring bounces, drawing up to where the others had congregated beyond the tall gates of the Keep.

Ian and Hillary did not linger atop Wallace. "Thank you, Wally," said Hillary. "You saved our lives and provided excellent service. How can we repay you?"

"I already gave the coins to that spiteful traitor of a master of yours," said Sir Godfrey, queasily unloading his valuables from the back of the wyvern he had ridden upon.

"Fear not," intoned one of the other wyverns. "The coins will no doubt still be there!"

"But what of you? Who will take care of you?" Hillary wanted to know.

"Don't bother your head about that yet, girl," said Godfrey. "They've still to take us back!" He swung his attention to Ian. "My goodness, Ian, this magic business is good for the complexion." He looked over to where Alison Gross was banging the doorknocker. "Why doesn't it do any good for her, then?"

The knights drew their swords, ready for anything.

Indeed, the walls of the castle did look the terrible old and forbidding sort, Ian thought. Riddled with the scars of ancient magic, no doubt. Ancient bare ivy vines covered the stone and mortar. Tattered flags flew above the gate like shreds of spitted souls.

"What now?" asked Hillary.

"It's all up to her, now, I suppose," Ian said, indicating the hag.

"Open up in there!" Alison Gross cried. "Hurry it up!"

The door opened. A butler—or rather, a bearlike creature wearing butler apparel—poked his head out. "My goodness," he said in a rich bass voice. "Our Alison has found her way back already! Shall I alert the master?"

"After you let us in, Parker!" Alison said.

Suddenly, a large dark form swooped down, blotting out the sun. It landed with a mighty flapping of wings and addressed the company with crossed arms. "That won't be necessary, Parker. This bunch isn't going anywhere."

Ian recognized him by his description. It was Princerik, the dragoon, majestically ugly, much larger in its reptilian attributes than the wyverns, who instinctively shrank back with fear. Ian was startled to see blossoms of smoke rising from the creature's nostrils—but a closer examination revealed that Princerik was not the fire-breathing variety of dragon, he was simply enjoying a gigantic cigar.

"Princerik, darling," said Alison Gross softly but sternly, swaying its way in a parody of sexiness. "You said I should find my way back!"

"I thought it would take years!" Princerik said, perceptibly softening. "Look, Alison, I'm in love with my Alandra, and she simply won't have you."

"Yes, and I understand the soft spot dragoons have in their hearts for—uh hum—virgin princesses," Alison declared in a reassuring, almost condescending voice. "And I realize that your mind was . . . clouded when you tossed me out. I will forgive you, Princerik. This is my home, and you are my dragoon." She gestured toward the knights. "But you must realize, my love, that virgin princesses are not without their higher purposes."

The dragoon squinted suspiciously. "And these dirtied knights here represent those higher purposes?"

"Indeed we do!" declared Sir Godfrey, striding forward manfully. "We, Lord Princerik, or whatever you call yourself, are the Holy Knights of Mullshire, on a quest for Alandra. I am told that I, Sir Godfrey of, er, Pinkham, am destined to be her savior, to carry her to that place where she might manifest her role as Key to this . . . uhm . . . dreadful mess that the world finds itself in!"

"Sounds quite romantic," said Princerik, "but I must say, I've only had her for a very short bit, and she is a fetching thing. Still, perhaps you are right. She doesn't seem terribly happy here . . . rather bored, I must say. And who am I to stand in the way of a holy mission? And I do rather miss Alison . . . as do the rest of the family."

The knights lowered their swords with disbelief. "No fight?"

In fact, to Ian it all seemed much too easy as well . . . but he wasn't going to question good fortune. If Princerik was going to give up Alandra so easily, then they should take her instantly and be gone, before the dragoon changed its mind. "There's nothing wrong with that!" he said cheerily.

"True," said Sir Mortimer. "Only it's rather an anticlimax after slogging through hell and losing three of our number!"

"Actually, I have some feisty beasties locked

away, if you'd care for some action," Princerik observed. "Just have to let them out of their chains. The guys have been saying they wouldn't mind a tasty knight tidbit."

"That's quite all right," said Sir Godfrey. "The boys have just had their heads jarred slightly in the journey, and will recover their senses after a good rest."

"Well, now, then, why don't you all come in and we'll have a nice talk? I merely have to go and find Alandra. She took herself off somewhere yesterday, and I'm not sure she's returned."

"Glad to see you're taking such good stock of your charge, Princerik," said Sir Godfrey. "Naturaly, we accept your hospitality. We trust you have suitable accommodations for our wyverns."

"Oh, I always have such for distant relatives! Come along then," said the dragoon. "Let them enter, Parker, and see that their needs are attended to. I'll wander off and have a talk with Alandra. She's the one who'll have the final say, of course."

"Just mention my name," said Sir Godfrey, beaming. "She'll come most joyfully when she hears her hero is here! And tell her though I have never met her in person, already I am totally in love with her majesty."

"Yes," Princerik agreed, "she is a lovable thing. But alas, I suppose that knights are more fitted to such as she than dragoons." He sighed, and, hands tucked in the pockets of his waistcoat, he slouched away to find Alandra.

They were shown to a waiting room by the very proper bearish butler. The room was filled with well-stuffed and high-backed chairs set upon an

ornate rug, surrounded by tables with all manner
of interesting bric-a-brac and differently shaped
mirrors. As the chairs were all man-sized and
quite comfortable-looking, the company promptly
selected seats and plopped down in them, the
knights utilizing the footstools with marked pleasure. Alison Gross bounced off happily to the
kitchens to see about tea and breakfast, while Sir
Godfrey Pinkham pulled the head of Kogar from
its bag and set it before him on a coffee table.

"We've not heard from this scoundrel for a
while," Sir Mortimer commented through half-
closed, resting eyes.

"No, and I'm worried," said Godfrey. "Now
that we don't have Alison to guide us, we don't
know where to go." He tapped the head. "Hallo,
in there. Hallo!"

The severed robot head's eyes remained blank.

Ian Farthing, settled in his chair beside Hillary's, was positively radiant with happiness. "I
did it, Hillary!" he said. "I've actually mended
my error! I've atoned for my mistake! I feel as
though . . . as though my soul has been set free!"

"Yes, Ian!" said Hillary, patting him gently on
his much-straightened hand. "That you have. But
don't forget, we have not finished with this business yet. We have to restore the princess to her
proper place and somehow set things to right—
and then we have to journey back to Mullshire."

"Yes!" said Ian. "Mullshire." A day or two ago,
the notion would have flooded him with anticipation and relief . . . but now, somehow, in his
different form he had a different attitude. He was
actually looking forward more to the resumption
of this adventure than to his return to the safety
of cobbling in his homeland.

How very strange, he thought, though he was not unpleased.

Tea arrived, but Princerik and Alandra remained absent.

Sir Oscar voiced concern, but was interrupted by Sir Godfrey's setting his cup down with a frightful clatter. "He's coming around!"

Sure enough, Ian saw, teacup halted halfway between saucer and lips, those black eyes within the head he had cut off had begun to glow. They opened, blinked, looked around. "By the Buddha's butt, you've made it," the voice ground out, full of static.

"Haven't heard from you lately, Roth Kogar," Sir Godfrey admonished the reformed Dark Lord.

"Yes. I have been having difficulties. . . . Things are unraveling even more in the Circle . . . difficult to use these methods to communicate."

"We're here, Kogar," said Godfrey. "We've made it to the castle where Alandra is being kept!"

Somehow, the eyes seemed to shine brighter. "Excellent! You have done well . . ." The voice sputtered. ". . . Alandra to . . ." And then the voice died.

"What did he say?" asked Sir William in his grumbly voice.

"Shhh!" said Godfrey. "It's fading back on!"

". . . and then . . ."

"Kogar!" said Godfrey. "Repeat the instructions, please!"

The voice came on suddenly full and strong. ". . . and there you must release me from my captivity! Only I have the secret of the place of Alandra's destiny! Only I . . ."

And then the voice died again.

"Well, that's it, then," said Sir Godfrey, shrugging. "Next stop, Kogar's castle. We'll just have to wait until he comes to so that he can tell us where that is!" He accepted more tea from the butler and sipped it with a self-satisfied smile. "Ah yes, within minutes, my own true darling love will waltz through that door, and she will be mine forever! Oh, it is a fine and noble thing to be a knightly hero. The traveling minstrels will get a lot of material out of this beautiful mythic romance, wouldn't you say, Sir Oscar?"

"I hope we live to relate the tale," Sir Oscar replied woefully, still green at the gills from airsickness.

"Now there's a thought. Oscar, you're a bit of a musician, aren't you? In the boring bits of this escapade, you might think about composing a song cycle about brave Sir Godfrey and his true love, the Princess Alandra. Yes, I think I should quite like that, and I daresay that my dear destined darling will heartily approve of the notion! And each of you, my faithful company, shall have your very own stanzas!"

Suddenly there was a commotion from without.

"Where are they?" an excited voice like the chime of bells demanded from down the hall.

A cat, beautifully golden and silver, bounded in and stopped short, taking in the assembled company with gleaming eyes.

"Oh joy of joys!" the cat cried, startling Ian with his capability for speech. "Knights! Our rescuers! Is it true?"

"And who are you?" Hillary asked, stepping forward, obviously charmed by this feline newcomer.

"And a darling princess as well!" the cat crooned in flattery, bouncing over and rubbing Hillary's shins languorously.

Hillary, delighted, bent down and picked up the cat, who immediately commenced to purr. "You are the most beautiful cat I have ever seen!"

The oaken door, partially ajar, suddenly was shoved all the way open. A young woman stood there, and behind her, Princerik hovered solicitously. "Here they are, Alandra. Will they do in the way of knightly rescuers, or should I toss them out?"

Ian stood, his heart pounding violently at the sight of Alandra. She was, if anything, more beautiful than he remembered from the time when she had bounded into his life through Jat's Pass. Instead of a gown, though, she wore snug breeches and a ruffled blouse that emphasized the excellence of her curves. She stood there, propped high on heeled riding boots, hands on hips, assaying the company before her. Her curly hair tumbled down like a waterfall of blond ecstasy . . . and her features, now slightly painted with makeup, made her more like a goddess than a mere princess or queen. The sight of her cut deep into Ian, causing his breathing to quicken.

At her side was a pouch; in her fingers she held a hand mirror.

"Took you long enough!" she snarled.

"Alandra?" Sir Godfrey cried, stepping forward, bending onto one knee, flinging open his arms in welcome. "It is I, Sir Godfrey Pinkham, come to rescue you at last!"

Alandra's eyes rested for a moment on Godfrey. "Oh," she said distractedly, gazing past him. "How nice." She strode forward.

Sir Godfrey's chest puffed out. His cheeks grew flushed with the pride of true chivalry rewarded. "Yes, my love! Take heart, for never more will you need fear—"

Alandra walked right past him, headed straight for Ian, gazing at him with a strange look in her wondrously blue eyes.

Oh no! thought Ian. She recognizes me! She's going to bash me on the head with that mirror!

And, indeed, Alandra had lifted her hand mirror up—a strangely sculpted affair—but instead of striking Ian, she tucked it into her leather belt. She stared at the lad, something like awe in her eyes.

"Oh brave new world," she said, "that has such creatures in it!"

Stunned, Ian glanced over his shoulder to see who she was talking to.

There was no one behind him.

Her entire face softened as she gazed upon Ian Farthing, her eyes going soft and misty.

"Oh, my hero," she said, taking his hand and placing it upon her cheek. "Say that I am thine forevermore."

Ian thought that he had died and gone to heaven as this gorgeous vision stared hopefully into his eyes.

"Hey! Just a goddam moment!" Sir Godfrey said indignantly. "I'm your hero! I'm Godfrey Pinkham!"

"Buzz off, bozo," she sneered. Then she directed another smile at Ian. "Oh darling, say that I might kiss your sweet lips before my heart yearns to breaking!"

Ian didn't know what to say, but before he

could even try he found Alandra's eager lips working on his, her delightful perfume threatening to engulf his senses.

It took a while, in which the entire company stared at this unexpected sight aghast, but finally Godfrey found his tongue.

"But Alandra! This is the idiot who caused your escape to fail!" he cried. "This is the dunce who has caused all your trouble!"

Alandra stepped away, shaking her head as though confused. "But how could that be? That fellow was a misshapen peasant, and I see before me a handsome, albeit quite short, man who grabs my heart with every gaze!"

"It's true," said Ian, having difficulty recovering his breath. "Alandra, it was I who caused your horse to fall into the quagmire. It was I who failed to stand against the Norx!"

He turned away, shamefaced.

Alandra sighed, her breast heaving quite splendidly. "Well, no one is perfect." She smiled and batted her lashes at Ian.

"This beats all!" said Godfrey, stamping about, clearly frustrated. "You work all your life to be a good knight, you grow strong and handsome and good, and then some rotten fink sneaks away with your destined princess!"

Hillary, too, seemed upset, frowning at the kissing. The cat, now in her arms, noticed immediately. "Ah! Is this your young man?"

"Well, no, not exactly," said Hillary, pouting.

"I shouldn't worry. That mirror she's carrying has been making her quite odd ever since she found it," the cat said. "Somehow, it makes her see things differently. But I sense that you seem to be a sane sort. My name is Alabaster."

"And mine is Hillary Muffin."

"Let's be good friends. Don't worry about Alandra. She's fickleness personified."

Ian, meanwhile, was not quite certain what had hit him. Alandra's touches, kisses, and caresses had his body tingly all over, his mind in a buzz. He felt swept away as though by some powerful spell. Why ever was this stunning specimen of womanhood so fascinated with him?

Truth to tell, though, Ian Farthing was much too besotted with the woman to question his good fortune.

"Yes, I shall be quite sorry to see those kisses go," said Princerik, wiping away a tear.

"I suggest," said Sir Oscar brightly, "that we take off immediately and thus waste no time!" He leaned over to the surly Sir Godfrey and whispered, "We shouldn't dawdle. This dragoon bloke might change its mind!"

"Right," said Sir William. "But where to? Shouldn't we wait until Lord Head here comes up with some travel directions?"

A shrieking sounded from the corridor beyond.

"Where is she?" cried a voice. "Where is that witch?"

"Uh oh," said Princerik. "Sounds like Alison is on the warpath." He smiled bleakly.

The hag stomped in, eyes afire. She had a look that Ian had never seen before. Where once had been cooperation, fear, and contriteness, now flamed an imperiousness, a deadly sternness making her ugliness far more striking and far more frightening. Her face had turned a mottled purple, and her yellowed teeth seemed somehow sharper.

Behind her was a three-tailed dog, teeth set into a rigid snarl.

"Oh! Hide me!" Alabaster hissed to Hillary, who responded quickly by tucking the cat under her cloak.

"My mirror!" Alison Gross cried. "My precious Mirror of Minos!" She pushed a crooked finger toward Alandra. "She stole it!"

"Mirror?" Alandra said, feigning innocence. "What mirror?"

"The one at your belt!" the hag replied promptly. "Now give it to me immediately!"

"I found it!" Alandra said. "It's mine now!"

"Found it? You blatant hussy, you arrogant whore!" screamed Alison. "You 'found' it by discovering the whereabouts of my room and upsetting poor Herbivorous terribly, destroying my dolls, then appropriating it. Princerik, that's mine! I demand that you have her return it to me!"

"Alandra, really," said Princerik. "Do you have to cause trouble?"

"It's mine now, and tough luck to you!" Alandra said haughtily. "Come, Ian, take me away from here."

"Princerikkkk!" Alison Gross cried. "Are you going to allow this . . . this blatant atrocity?"

Princerik threw its hands up in dismay. "I have nothing to do with this! My nerves are entirely too frayed as it is!" It winked over to Alandra. "And a successful journey to you, my dear! I'm going to my library for a restful read."

And with that, the dragoon departed with a faint flutter of its wings, a slight whipping of its coattails.

The hag was outraged.

"Gentlemennnnn!" she said. "I took you here. I

brought you to your destination. Now all I ask is that you have this . . . this creature return what is rightfully mine."

"Oh dear hero, Ian," said Alandra. "And gentle good knights! I feel somehow that this mirror is of utmost importance in my life's most holy mission." She batted her eyes prettily. "How can I return it to this . . . scumbag?"

"Come now, Alison," Sir Godfrey said after gazing at Alandra wistfully. "Take some coins for your paltry ornament so that we may go peaceably. Surely you don't want to look at yourself anyway. Come, fellows, let's begone from this place. We have a mission to continue."

"Over my dead body!" Alison Gross shrieked.

"That can be arranged," replied Godfrey, drawing his sword.

Herbivorous growled.

Alison Gross turned apoplectic, her curses garbled with her rage. When she finally recovered her tongue, she cried, "You do not understand, you lame-brained knight! Outside, I lacked in defenses . . ."

"Though surely not in offensiveness!" put in Alandra.

". . . but I foresaw this eventuality," continued the hag, "in my Crystal Bowel, and have brought allies from beneath to help me present my case!"

She put her fingers to her lips and gave a shrill blast of a whistle.

Herbivorous wagged its tails and seemed to smile smugly.

Almost immediately, the doorway was thronged by a menagerie of monsters. Fangs clicked and tentacles lashed. Teeth gleamed and claws clacked on the stone floor. Nameless creatures drooled and undulated behind the hag.

"I'm certainly glad I didn't stumble across those guys downstairs," Alandra sniffed.

"Beside those, that hag does look beautiful," said Sir Mortimer. "May I suggest we not belabor the situation by lingering?"

Fortunately, there was a door on the other side of the room.

The company sprinted for it.

Somehow they managed to squeeze through the door, several at a time.

Ian almost found himself trampled in the rush, pounded by chain mail, bumped by elbows and sword pommels. The knights charged through the hallway pell-mell, causing enough din to raise the dead ... in this kind of place a definite possibility.

Ian ventured a breathless look behind him. As he was last in the race toward the courtyard, he thought he might protect the flanks by utilizing his magical sword-pen. But he found himself confronted by such a frightful collection of hobgoblins that wisdom got the better of his temporary valor and he decided running away would be best for all involved.

"Get them!" Alison Gross cried vengefully. "I must have that mirror back!"

Her minions crawled and flopped along in obedience, oozing and drooling.

Fortunately, the frontmost fright tripped over some obscenely dangling appendages and the pursuing creatures tripped and tumbled over one another, giving the questers a few spare moments.

The wyverns were waiting where they had been placed, munching on their breakfast crumpets and

slurping buckets of tea. Wallace Wyvern's eye
shot open at the sight of the group clamoring
toward them so recklessly and hastily.

"What gives?" he inquired politely.

"We've got to leave!" said Hillary, hopping atop
his back. "Fast! No time for explanations!"

"But where to?" the wyvern said, blinking with
surprise.

"Up!" cried Hillary as Alabaster clung to her
for dear life, eyes wide and terrified.

The knights speedily mounted, urging the winged
steeds in the same direction. Alandra selected
one and jumped on as though this was all second
nature to her. Blithely, she motioned for the lag-
ging Ian to share her wyvern. He hurried there,
puffing, making no objection.

The grimoire's worth of creatures spewed from
the door under the urgent direction of Alison
Gross.

Wyvern wings spread.

"Off!" Alandra commanded imperiously.

The wings flapped. Mighty legs pushed off from
the ground. Soon all the wyverns were safely
aloft, leaving behind the jabbers and jumps of
their pursuers, mixed with the frustrated cries of
Alison Gross.

"May that mirror be your curse, Alandra!" the
hag yelled.

Alandra looked down at the dwindling lump
that was Alison Gross and, with a fruity Bronx
cheer, thumbed her nose.

Ian was enchanted. What unorthodox behavior
from a princess! How engaging!

After gaining elevation, the wyverns followed
Wallace, their leader, though to where Ian Farthing had no idea.

Alandra seemed not to be distressed at all about not knowing where they were going. As their wyvern sailed through the sun-golden skies at an elevation affording a spectacular view of the twisting and turning landscape of the Dark Circle, almost twinkling now with its magicks, Alandra seemed preoccupied, holding on to her reins with one hand and contemplating herself in the mirror.

"The Mirror of Minos, Alison called it," said Ian Farthing above the roar of the winds. He looked at the hand mirror, noticing the dice faces inlaid on the handle. A tingle touched his spine. "What's so special about it, Alandra?"

"I haven't the faintest, my darling rescuer," returned the beauty. "I just like the way it makes me look."

She angled the mirror so that Ian could see her reflection. Ian's breath was almost taken away. For somehow, in this oval looking glass, Alandra's loveliness was amplified, her beauty perfect and everlasting.

A tear dropped from Ian's eye ... but as he looked closer in the mirror, the clouds above seemed to move, collecting into what seemed the face of a man, with stars as eyes. . . .

A star-eye winked at him, and then the illusion wisped away into the mirror-sky.

Ian closed his eyes and swallowed softly, trying to control the fear that seemed to shake the fibers of his being, threatening to engulf him in a fit that would surely plummet him from the wyvern.

For he had seen that face before, in his darkest nightmares.

And perhaps, somewhere else, long ago, so very long ago. . . .

When he had recovered, he leaned his head sorrowfully against Alandra's back.

"Something wrong, Ian?" said Alandra.

"I have the feeling," Ian Farthing said, "that we have a long way to go before this is through. A very long way."

He sighed and gazed at the dice-shaped moon rising up on a curved horizon, like him just another playing piece in an eternal mysterious game.

About the Author

DAVID F. BISCHOFF was born December 15, 1951, in Washington, D.C., and grew up in the D.C. suburbs carousing with Air Force brats near Andrews AFB. He graduated from the University of Maryland in 1973 with a B.A. in TV and Film and worked for six years with NBC Washington, then became a full-time free-lance writer.

He has written a number of novels, including *Night-world*, *Star Fall*, *Mandala*, *Day of the Dragonstar* (with Thomas F. Monteleone), *The Selkie* (with Charles Shef-field; available in a Signet edition), and the upcoming *Infinite Battle* and *Cosmos Computer*. *The Destiny Dice*, Book one of two volumes of *The Gaming Magi* is also available in a Signet edition.

His short work has appeared in such magazines as *Omni*, *Analog*, *Fantasy & Science Fiction*, and *Amazing*, as well as a number of original anthologies.

He has served as both secretary and vice-president of the Science Fiction Writers of America.

Bischoff loves movies, rock and British folk, and other things too humorous to mention. He now lives in Silver Spring, Maryland.

JOIN THE *GAMING MAGI* READERS' PANEL

Help us bring you more of the books you like by filling out this survey and mailing it in today.

1. Book Title: _____
   Book #: _____

2. Using the scale below, how would you rate this book on the following features?

		NOT SO								EXCEL-
POOR		GOOD		O.K.			GOOD			LENT
0	1	2	3	4	5	6	7	8	9	10

RATING

Overall opinion of book .... _____
Plot/Story .... _____
Setting/Location .... _____
Writing Style .... _____
Character Development .... _____
Conclusion/Ending .... _____
Scene on Front Cover .... _____

3. On average about how many books do you buy for yourself each month? _____

4. How would you classify yourself as a reader of SF/Fantasy? I am a ( ) light ( ) medium ( ) heavy reader.

5. What is your education?
   ( ) High School (or less) ( ) 4 yrs. college
   ( ) 2 yrs. college ( ) Post Graduate

6. Age _____ 7. Sex: ( ) Male ( ) Female

8. Please Print Name:_____

   Address:_____

   City: _____ State: _____ Zip: _____

   Phone #: ( )_____

Thank you. Please send to New American Library, Research Dept., 1633 Broadway, New York, NY 10019.